the general zapped an angel

SHORT STORY COLLECTIONS BY HOWARD FAST

Patrick Henry and the Frigate's Keel, and Other Stories of a Young Nation (1945)

Departure, and Other Stories (1949)

The Last Supper and Other Stories (1955)

The Howard Fast Reader: A Collection of Stories and Novels (1960)

The Edge of Tomorrow (1961)

The Hunter and The Trap (1967)

The General Zapped an Angel (1970)

A Touch of Infinity (1973)

Time and the Riddle: Thirty-One Zen Stories (1975)

The Call of Fife and Drum: Three Novels of the Revolution (1987)

ECCO ART OF THE STORY

The Delicate Prey by Paul Bowles

Catastrophe by Dino Buzzati

The Essential Tales of Chekhov by Anton Chekhov

Whatever Happened to Interracial Love? by Kathleen Collins

Continent by Jim Crace

The Vanishing Princess by Jenny Diski

The Garden Party by Katherine Mansfield

Wild Nights! by Joyce Carol Oates

Mr. and Mrs. Baby by Mark Strand

In the Garden of the North American Martyrs by Tobias Wolff

Lucky Girls by Nell Freudenberger

Hue and Cry by James Alan McPherson

the general zapped an angel

STORIES

howard fast

HarperCollins books may be purchased for educational, business, or sales promotional use. For information, please email the Special Markets Department at SPsales@harpercollins.com.

Originally published in 1969 by Ace Books, a division of Charter Communications Inc., by arrangement with William Morrow & Co., Inc.

FIRST ECCO PAPERBACK EDITION PUBLISHED 2019.

Designed by Michelle Crowe
Background Texture on Title Page by Ethnic Design /Shutterstock, Inc.

Library of Congress Cataloging-in-Publication Data has been applied for.

ISBN 978-0-06-290844-5

19 20 21 22 23 LSC 10 9 8 7 6 5 4 3 2 1

contents

For Rachel and Paul:
Greetings

preface

by Mark Harris

In 1950, Joseph McCarthy tried to silence Howard Fast. It was a fool's errand. Called to testify before the House Un-American Activities Committee, Fast refused to name names, served three months in prison for contempt of Congress, and had to resort for some time to a pseudonym to survive the blacklist. It was scarcely a speed bump in a career of astonishing variety and prolificity. Fast was a novelist, an essayist, a poet, a playwright, a young adult author before that was even a named genre (his *April Morning* was a staple of middle school curricula for decades), a biographer, an autobiographer, and, as this volume attests, a short story writer. Something like one hundred books bore his name (or one of his aliases). His first novel was published in 1933, when he was eighteen, and his pace barely abated for the next seventy years. Even in prison, Fast didn't take a break; he started what would become one of his most famous novels, *Spartacus*, self-publishing it to great success upon his release. He wrote—including, during the blacklist years, for the *Daily Worker*—like it was a job and a calling. And he wore his politics on his sleeve.

By the time this delightful, imaginative, irate collection was published in 1970, those politics had evolved, but not mellowed. Fast was no longer a Communist, having become disillusioned with Stalin in the early 1950s, but his rage at American militarism, greed, and profiteering did not abate, and it resounds through these nine stories like a hand pounded on a breakfast table over strong black coffee and the morning paper. This collection offers a mix of sci-fi, fantasy, horror, and dystopian black comedy, a combination of moods that emerged from a political moment when U.S. involvement in the Vietnam War was the subject of daily household argument, and from a cultural moment when *Star Trek* had recently merged speculative fiction with liberal social consciousness and brought the results into American homes.

Fast leapt genres, tones, and styles to suit his interests. In the title story, an American general in Vietnam who began his assaultive career by killing puppies works his way up to shooting an actual angel out of the sky; it's a savage portrayal of military swagger and heedlessness, the prose equivalent of a satirical protest song. "Tomorrow's *Wall Street Journal*" features a guest appearance by the devil, who—Fast would have it no other way—naturally self-identifies as a conservative. In "The Mouse," visitors from another planet land their small flying saucer in a suburban yard, imbue a mouse with the consciousness of a human, and leave him in suicidal despair, the only rational response to a world that, for the first time, he now understands.

The stories in *The General Zapped an Angel* are not subtle, fussed-over pieces of prose. Straightforward and blunt, most of them read like a good day's (or a good few days') work, written in plain English to get the point across. Fast did not suffer from writer's block or a lack of ideas. His 2003 *New York Times* obituary quotes him as saying, "The only thing that infuriates me is that I have more unwritten stories in me than I can conceivably write in a lifetime." It didn't take much to get him started—these pieces are, for the most part, a whim or a wince or a grin or a grimace at the state of the world spun into brisk narrative. But cumulatively, they offer readers a powerful, plaintive kind of undertow: they have the feel of religious parables, recognizably Jewish in their rhythm and their stretchiness, their shrugging joke structure and their moral rigor, their humor and their outrage. Their sense of futility feels bone-deep, the product of a life's contemplation of mankind racing toward the edge of a cliff.

Because many of these stories are the product of their historical moment, it's jolting to see that their subject matter is anything but quaint. One can't exactly laugh off "The Wound," in which nuclear weapons are reimagined as the latest (and last) tool of oilmen looking for a new way to dislodge deposits beneath the earth's surface—it's a heart's cry that is no less resonant today than it was half a century ago. (Does anyone doubt what Fast would have to say about fracking?)

And in at least one case, Fast appears to have had the assistance of a time machine. "The Vision of Milty Boil" tells the story of a powerful New York City real estate tycoon—a man obsessed with amassing power and wealth who, despite being derided as an idiot by the skeptics around him, proceeds to remake the cityscape in ways systematically designed to make himself larger and everybody else smaller. In this mordantly funny little masterpiece, bedrooms, buildings, even humanity itself can all be tailored to soothe the insecurity and enhance the vanity of a man who absolutely does not want to be seen as small. Fast follows Milty into the 1980s, the 1990s, and beyond, finally crafting an epitaph that is perfect for him and just as apt for us. Like many of the stories in *The General Zapped an Angel*, it's a nightmare that eventually releases us back into our own reality with the snap of a bitter little joke. And there is particular pleasure in unearthing it fifty years after it last occupied Fast's mind.

To read these stories is to open a time capsule prepared by a man who could not have imagined what the world would become and yet, as often as not, managed to take a pretty impressive guess.

the

general

zapped

an

angel

the general zapped an angel

When news leaked out of Viet Nam that Old Hell and Hardtack Mackenzie had shot down an angel, every newspaper in the world dug into its morgue for the background and biography of this hard-bitten old warrior.

Not that General Clayborne Mackenzie was so old. He had only just passed his fiftieth birthday, and he had plenty of piss and vinegar left in him when he went out to Viet Nam to head up the 55th Cavalry and its two hundred helicopters; and the sight of him sitting in the open door of a gunship, handling a submachine gun like the pro he was, and zapping anything that moved there below—because anything that moved was likely enough to be Charlie—had inspired many a fine color story.

Correspondents liked to stress the fact that Mackenzie was a "natural fighting man," with, as they put it, "an instinct for the kill." In this they were quite right, as the material from the various newspaper morgues proved. When Mackenzie was only six years old, playing in the yard of his North Carolina home, he managed to kill a puppy by beating it to death with a stone, an extraordinary act of courage and perseverance. After that, he was able to earn spending money by killing unwanted puppies and kittens for five cents each. He was an intensely creative child, one of the things that contributed to his subsequent leadership qualities, and not content with drowning the animals, he devised five other methods for destroying the unwanted pets. By nine he was trapping rabbits and rats and had invented a unique yet simple mole trap that caught the moles alive. He enjoyed turning over live moles and mice to neighborhood cats, and often he would invite his little playmates to watch the results. At the age of twelve his father gave him his first gun—and from there on no one who knew young Clayborne Mackenzie doubted either his future career or success.

After his arrival in Viet Nam, there was no major mission of the 55th that Old Hell and Hardtack did not lead in person. The sight of him blazing away from the gunship became a symbol of the "new war," and the troops on the ground would look for him and up at him and cheer him when he appeared. (Sometimes the cheers were earthy, but that is only to be expected in war.) There was nothing Mackenzie loved better than a village full of skulking, treacherous VC, and once he passed over such a village, little was left of it. A young newspaper correspondent compared him to an "avenging angel," and sometimes when his helicopters were called in to help a group of hard-pressed infantry, he thought of himself in such terms. It was on just such an occasion, when the company of marines holding the outpost at Quen-to were so hard pressed, that the thing happened.

General Clayborne Mackenzie had led the attack, blazing away, and down came the angel, square into the marine encampment. It took a while for them to realize what they had, and Mackenzie had already returned to base field when the call came from Captain Joe Kelly, who was in command of the marine unit.

"General, sir," said Captain Kelly, when Mackenzie had picked up the phone and asked what in hell they wanted, "General Mackenzie, sir, it would seem that you shot down an angel."

"Say that again, Captain."

"An angel, sir."

"A what?"

"An angel, sir."

"And just what in hell is an angel?"

"Well," Kelly answered, "I don't quite know how to answer that, sir. An angel is an angel. One of God's angels, sir."

"Are you out of your goddamn mind, Captain?" Mackenzie roared. "Or are you sucking pot again? So help me God, I warned you potheads that if you didn't lay off the grass I would see you all in hell!"

"No, sir," said Kelly quietly and stubbornly. "We have no pot here."

"Well, put on Lieutenant Garcia!" Mackenzie yelled.

"Lieutenant Garcia." The voice came meekly.

"Lieutenant, what the hell is this about an angel?"

"Yes, General."

"Yes, what?"

"It is an angel. When you were over here zapping VC—well, sir, you just went and zapped an angel."

"So help me God," Mackenzie yelled, "I will break every one of you potheads for this! You got a lot of guts, buster, to put on a full general, but nobody puts me on and walks away from it. Just remember that."

One thing about Old Hell and Hardtack, when he wanted something done, he didn't ask for volunteers. He did it himself, and now he went to his helicopter and told Captain Jerry Gates, the pilot:

"You take me out to that marine encampment at Quen-to and put me right down in the middle of it."

"It's a risky business, General."

"It's your goddamn business to fly this goddamn ship and not to advise me."

Twenty minutes later the helicopter settled down into the encampment at Quen-to, and a stony-faced full general faced Captain Kelly and said:

"Now suppose you just lead me to that damn angel, and God help you if it's not."

But it was; twenty feet long and all of it angel, head to foot. The marines had covered it over with two tarps, and it was their good luck that the VCs either had given up on Quen-to or had simply decided not to fight for a while—because there was not much fight left in the marines, and all the young men could do was to lay in their holes and try not to look at the big body under the two tarps and not to talk about it either; but in spite of how they tried, they kept sneaking glances at it and they kept on whispering about it, and the two of them who pulled off the tarps so that General Mackenzie might see began to cry a little. The general didn't like that; if there was one thing he did not like, it was soldiers who cried, and he snapped at Kelly:

"Get these two mothers the hell out of here, and when you assign a detail to me, I want men, not wet-nosed kids." Then he surveyed the angel, and even he was impressed.

"It's a big son of a bitch, isn't it?"

"Yes, sir. Head to heel, it's twenty feet. We measured it."

"What makes you think it's an angel?"

"Well, that's the way it is," Kelly said. "It's an angel. What else is it?"

General Mackenzie walked around the recumbent form and had to admit the logic in Captain Kelly's thinking. The thing was white, not flesh-white but snow-white, shaped like a man, naked, and sprawled on its side with two great feathered wings folded under it. Its hair was spun gold and its face was too beautiful to be human.

"So that's an angel," Mackenzie said finally.

"Yes, sir."

"Like hell it is!" Mackenzie snorted. "What I see is a white, Caucasian male, dead of wounds suffered on the field of combat. By the way, where'd I hit him?"

"We can't find the wounds, sir."

"Now just what the hell do you mean, you can't find the wounds? I don't miss. If I shot it, I shot it."

"Yes, sir. But we can't find the wounds. Perhaps its skin is very tough. It might have been the concussion that knocked it down."

Used to getting at the truth of things himself, Mackenzie walked up and down the body, going over it carefully. No wounds were visible.

"Turn the angel over," Mackenzie said.

Kelly, who was a good Catholic, hesitated at first; but between a live general and a dead angel, the choice was specified. He called out a detail of marines, and without enthusiasm they managed to turn over the giant body. When Mackenzie complained that mud smears were impairing his inspection, they wiped the angel clean. There were no wounds on this side either.

"That's a hell of a note," Mackenzie muttered, and if Captain Kelly and Lieutenant Garcia had been more familiar with the moods of Old Hell and Hardtack, they would have heard a tremor of uncertainty in his voice. The truth is that Mackenzie was just a little baffled. "Anyway," he decided, "it's dead, so wrap it up and put it in the ship."

"Sir?"

"Goddamnit, Kelly, how many times do I have to give you an order? I said, wrap it up and put it in the ship!"

The marines at Quen-to were relieved as they watched Mackenzie's gunship disappear in the distance, preferring the company of live VCs to that of a dead angel, but the pilot of the helicopter flew with all the assorted worries of a Southern Fundamentalist.

"Is that sure enough an angel, sir?" he had asked the general.

"You mind your eggs and fly the ship, son," the general replied. An hour ago he would have told the pilot to keep his goddamn nose out of things that didn't concern him, but the angel had a stultifying effect on the general's language. It depressed him, and when the three-star general at headquarters said to him, "Are you trying to tell me, Mackenzie, that you shot down an angel?" Mackenzie could only nod his head miserably.

"Well, sir, you are out of your goddamn mind."

"The body's outside in Hangar F," said Mackenzie. "I put a guard over it, sir."

The two-star general followed the three-star general as he stalked to Hangar F, where the three-star general looked at the body, poked it with his toe, poked it with his finger, felt the feathers, felt the hair, and then said:

"Goddamnit to hell, Mackenzie, do you know what you got here?"

"Yes, sir."

"You got an angel—that's what the hell you got here."

"Yes, sir, that's the way it would seem."

"God damn you, Mackenzie, I always had a feeling that I should have put my foot down instead of letting you zoom up and down out there in those gunships zapping VCs. My God almighty, you're supposed to be a grown man with some sense instead of some dumb kid who wants to make a score zapping Charlie, and if you hadn't been out there in that gunship this would never have happened. Now what in hell am I supposed to do? We got a lousy enough press on this war. How am I going to explain a dead angel?"

"Maybe we don't explain it, sir. I mean, there it is. It happened. The damn thing's dead, isn't it? Let's bury it. Isn't that what a soldier does—buries his dead, tightens his belt a notch, and goes on from there?"

"So we bury it, huh, Mackenzie?"

"Yes, sir. We bury it."

"You're a horse's ass, Mackenzie. How long since someone told you that? That's the trouble with being a general in this goddamn army—no one ever gets to tell you what a horse's ass you are. You got dignity."

"No, sir. You're not being fair, sir," Mackenzie protested. "I'm trying to help. I'm trying to be creative in this trying situation."

"You get a gold star for being creative, Mackenzie. Yes, sir,

General—that's what you get. Every marine at Quen-to knows you shot down an angel. Your helicopter pilot and crew know it, which means that by now everyone on this base knows it—because anything that happens here, I know it last—and those snotnose reporters on the base, they know it, not to mention the goddamn chaplains, and you want to bury it. Bless your heart."

The three-star general's name was Drummond, and when he got back to his office, his aide said to him excitedly:

"General Drummond, sir, there's a committee of chaplains, sir, who insist on seeing you, and they're very up tight about something, and I know how you feel about chaplains, but this seems to be something special, and I think you ought to see them."

"I'll see them." General Drummond sighed.

There were four chaplains, a Catholic priest, a rabbi, an Episcopalian, and a Lutheran. The Methodist, Baptist, and Presbyterian chaplains had wanted to be a part of the delegation, but the priest, who was a Paulist, said that if they were to bring in five Protestants, he wanted a Jesuit as reenforcement, while the rabbi, who was Reform, agreed that against five Protestants an Orthodox rabbi ought to join the Jesuit. The result was a compromise, and they agreed to allow the priest, Father Peter O'Malley, to talk for the group. Father O'Malley came directly to the point:

"Our information is, General, that General Mackenzie has shot down one of God's holy angels. Is that or is that not so?"

"I'm afraid it's so," Drummond admitted.

There was a long moment of silence while the collective clergy gathered its wits, its faith, its courage, and its astonishment, and then Father O'Malley asked slowly and ominously:

"And what have you done with the body of this holy creature, if indeed it has a body?"

"It has a body—a very substantial body. In fact, it's as large as a young elephant, twenty feet tall. It's lying in Hangar F, under guard."

Father O'Malley shook his head in horror, looked at his Protestant colleagues, and then passed over them to the rabbi and said to him:

"What are your thoughts, Rabbi Bernstein?"

Since Rabbi Bernstein represented the oldest faith that was concerned with angels, the others deferred to him.

"I think we ought to look upon it immediately," the rabbi said.

"I agree," said Father O'Malley.

The other clergy joined in this agreement, and they repaired to Hangar F, a journey not without difficulty, for by now the press had come to focus on the story, and the general and the clergy ran a sort of gauntlet of pleading questions as they made their way on foot to Hangar F. The guards there barred the press, and the clergy entered with General Drummond and General Mackenzie and half a dozen other staff officers. The angel was uncovered, and the men made a circle around the great, beautiful thing, and then for almost five minutes there was silence.

Father O'Malley broke the silence. "God forgive us," he said.

There was a circle of amens, and then more silence, and finally Whitcomb, the Episcopalian, said:

"It could conceivably be a natural phenomenon."

Father O'Malley looked at him wordlessly, and Rabbi Bernstein softened the blow with the observation that even God and His holy angels could be considered as not apart from nature, whereupon Pastor Yager, the Lutheran, objected to a pantheistic viewpoint at a time like this, and Father O'Malley snapped:

"The devil with this theological nonsense! The plain fact of the matter is that we are standing in front of one of God's holy angels, which we in our animal-like sinfulness have slain. What penance we must do is more to the point."

"Penance is your field, gentlemen," said General Drummond. "I have the problem of a war, the press, and this body."

"This body, as you call it," said Father O'Malley, "obviously should be sent to the Vatican—immediately, if you ask me."

"Oh, ho!" snorted Whitcomb. "The Vatican! No discussion, no exchange of opinion—oh, no, just ship it off to the Vatican where it can be hidden in some secret dungeon with any other evidence of God's divine favor—"

"Come now, come now," said Rabbi Bernstein soothingly. "We are witness to something very great and holy, and we should not argue as to where this holy thing of God belongs. I think it is obvious that it belongs in Jerusalem."

While this theological discussion raged, it occurred to General Clayborne Mackenzie that his own bridges needed mending, and he stepped outside to where the press—swollen by now to almost the entire press corps in Viet Nam—waited, and of course they grabbed him.

"Is it true, General?"

"Is what true?"

"Did you shoot down an angel?"

"Yes, I did," the old warrior stated forthrightly.

"For heaven's sake, why?" asked a woman photographer.

"It was a mistake," said Old Hell and Hardtack modestly.

"You mean you didn't see it?" asked another voice.

"No, sir. Peripheral, if you know what I mean. I was in the gunship zapping Charlie, and bang–there it was."

The press was skeptical. A dozen questions came, all to the point of how he knew that it was an angel.

"You don't ask why a river's a river, or a donkey's a donkey," Mackenzie said bluntly. "Anyway, we have professional opinion inside."

Inside, the professional opinion was divided and angry. All were agreed that the angel was a sign–but what kind of a sign was another matter entirely. Pastor Yager held that it was a sign for peace, calling for an immediate cease-fire. Whitcomb, the Episcopalian, held, however, that it was merely a condemnation of indiscriminate zapping, while the rabbi and the priest held that it was a sign–period. Drummond said that sooner or later the press must be allowed in and that the network men must be permitted to put the dead angel on television. Whitcomb and the rabbi agreed. O'Malley and Yager demurred. General Robert L. Robert of the Engineer Corps arrived with secret information that the whole thing was a put-on by the Russians and that the angel was a robot, but when they attempted to cut the flesh to see whether the angel bled or not, the skin proved to be impenetrable.

At that moment the angel stirred, just a trifle, yet enough to make the clergy and brass gathered around him leap back to give him room–for that gigantic twenty-foot form, weighing better than half a ton, was one thing dead and something else entirely alive. The angel's biceps were as thick around as a man's body, and his great, beautiful head was mounted on a neck almost a yard in diameter. Even the clerics were sufficiently hazy on angelology to be at all certain that even an angel might not resent being shot down. As he stirred a second time, the men around him moved even farther away, and some of the brass nervously loosened their sidearms.

"If this holy creature is alive," Rabbi Bernstein said bravely, "then he will have neither hate nor anger toward us. His nature is of love and forgiveness. Don't you agree with me, Father O'Malley?"

If only because the Protestant ministers were visibly dubious, Father O'Malley agreed. "By all means. Oh, yes."

"Just how the hell do you know?" demanded General Drummond, loosening his sidearm. "That thing has the strength of a bulldozer."

Not to be outdone by a combination of Catholic and Jew, Whitcomb stepped forward bravely and faced Drummond and said, "That 'thing,' as you call it, sir, is one of the Almighty's blessed angels, and you would do better to see to your immortal soul than to your sidearm."

To which Drummond yelled, "Just who the hell do you think you are talking to, mister—just—"

At that moment the angel sat up, and the men around him leaped away to widen the circle. Several drew their sidearms; others whispered whatever prayers they could remember. The angel, whose eyes were as blue as the skies over Viet Nam when the monsoon is gone and the sun shines through the washed air, paid almost no attention to them at first. He opened one wing and then the other, and his great wings almost filled the hangar. He flexed one arm and then the other, and then he stood up.

On his feet, he glanced around him, his blue eyes moving steadily from one to another, and when he did not find what he sought, he walked to the great sliding doors of Hangar F and spread them open with a single motion. To the snapping of steel regulators and the grinding of stripped gears, the doors parted—revealing to the crowd outside, newsmen, officers, soldiers, and civilians, the mighty, twenty-foot-high, shining form of the angel.

No one moved. The sight of the angel, bent forward slightly, his splendid wings half spread, not for flight but to balance him, held them hypnotically fixed, and the angel himself moved his eyes from face to face, finding finally what he sought—none other than Old Hell and Hardtack Mackenzie.

As in those Western films where the moment of "truth," as they call it, is at hand, where sheriff and badman stand face to face, their hands twitching over their guns—as the crowd melts away from the two marked men in those films, so did the crowd melt away from around Mackenzie until he stood alone—as alone as any man on earth.

The angel took a long, hard look at Mackenzie, and then the angel sighed and shook his head. The crowd parted for him as he walked past Mackenzie and down the field—where, squarely in the middle of Runway Number 1, he spread his mighty wings and took off, the way an eagle leaps from his perch into the sky, or—as some reporters put it—as a dove flies gently.

the mouse

Only the mouse watched the flying saucer descend to earth. The mouse crouched apprehensively in a mole's hole, its tiny nose twitching, its every nerve quivering in fear and attention as the beautiful golden thing made a landing.

The flying saucer—or circular spaceship, shaped roughly like a flattened, wide-brimmed hat—slid past the roof of the split-level suburban house, swam across the back yard, and then settled into a tangle of ramblers, nestling down among the branches and leaves so that it was covered entirely. And since the flying saucer was only about thirty inches in diameter and no more than seven inches in height, the camouflage was accomplished rather easily.

It was just past three o'clock in the morning. The inhabitants of this house and of all the other houses in this particular suburban development slept or tossed in their beds and struggled with insomnia. The passage of the flying saucer was soundless and without odor, so no dog barked; only the mouse watched—and he watched without comprehension, even as he always watched, even as his existence was—without comprehension.

What had just happened became vague and meaningless in the memory of the mouse—for he hardly had a memory at all. It might never have happened. Time went by, seconds, minutes, almost an hour, and then a light appeared in the tangle of briars and leaves where the saucer lay. The mouse fixed on the light, and then he saw two men appear, stepping out of the light, which was an opening into the saucer, and onto the ground.

Or at least they appeared to be vaguely like creatures the mouse had seen that actually were men—except that they were only three inches tall and enclosed in spacesuits. If the mouse could have distinguished between the suit and what it contained and if the mouse's vision had been selective, he might have seen that under the transparent covering the men from the saucer differed only in size from the men on earth—at least in general appearance. Yet in other ways they differed a great deal. They did not speak vocally, nor did their suits contain any sort of radio equipment; they were telepaths, and after they had stood in silence for about five minutes they exchanged thoughts.

"The thing to keep in mind," said the first man, "is that while our weight is so much less here than at home, we are still very, very heavy. And this ground is not very dense."

"No, it isn't, is it? Are they all asleep?"

The first reached out. His mind became an electronic network that touched the minds of every living creature within a mile or so.

"Almost all of the people are asleep. Most of the animals appear to be nocturnal."

"Curious."

"No—not really. Most of the animals are undomesticated—small, wild creatures. Great fear—hunger and fear."

"Poor things."

"Yes—poor things, yet they manage to survive. That's quite a feat, under the noses of the people. Interesting people. Probe a bit."

The second man reached out with his mind and probed. His reaction might be translated as "Ugh!"

"Yes—yes, indeed. They think some horrible thoughts, don't they? I'm afraid I prefer the animals. There's one right up ahead of us. Wide awake and with nothing else in that tiny brain of his but fear. In fact, fear and hunger seem to add up to his total mental baggage. Not hate, no aggression."

"He's also quite small as things go on this planet," the second spaceman observed. "No larger than we are. You know, he might just do for us."

"He might," the first agreed.

With that, the two tiny men approached the mouse, who still crouched defensively in the mole hole, only the tip of its whiskered nose showing. The two men moved very slowly and carefully, choosing their steps with great deliberation. One of them suddenly sank almost to his knees in a little bit of earth, and after that they attempted to find footing on stones, pebbles, bits of wood. Evidently their great weight made the hard, dry earth too soft for safety. Meanwhile the mouse watched them, and when their direction became evident, the mouse attempted the convulsive action of escape.

But his muscles would not respond, and as panic seared his small brain, the first spaceman reached into the mouse's mind, soothing him, finding the fear center and blocking it off with his own thoughts and then electronically shifting the mouse's neuron paths to the pleasure centers of the tiny animal's brain. All this the spacemen did effortlessly and almost instantaneously, and the mouse relaxed, made squeaks of joy, and gave up any attempt to escape. The second spaceman then broke the dirt away from the tunnel mouth, lifted the mouse with ease, holding him in his arms, and carried him back to the saucer. And the mouse lay there, relaxed and cooing with delight.

Two others, both women, were waiting in the saucer as the men came through the air lock, carrying the mouse. The women—evidently in tune with the men's thoughts—did not have to be told what had happened. They had prepared what could only be an operating table, a flat panel of bright light overhead and a board of instruments alongside. The light made a square of brilliance in the darkened interior of the spaceship.

"I am sterile," the first woman informed the men, holding up hands encased in thin, transparent gloves, "so we can proceed immediately."

Like the men, the women's skin was yellow, not sallow but a bright, glowing lemon yellow, the hair rich orange. Out of the spacesuits, they would all be dressed more or less alike, barefoot and in shorts in the warm interior of the ship; nor did the women cover their well-formed breasts.

"I reached out," the second woman told them. "They're all asleep, but their minds!"

"We know," the men agreed.

"I rooted around—like a journey through a sewer. But I picked up a good deal. The animal is called a mouse. It is symbolically the smallest and most harmless of creatures, vegetarian, and hunted by practically everything else on this curious planet. Only its size accounts for its survival, and its only skill is in concealment."

Meanwhile the two men had laid the mouse on the operating table, where it sprawled relaxed and squeaking contentment. While the men went to change out of their spacesuits, the second woman filled a hypodermic instrument, inserted the needle near the base of the mouse's tail, and gently forced the fluid in. The mouse relaxed and became unconscious. Then the two women changed the mouse's position, handling the—to them huge—animal with ease and dispatch, as if it had almost no weight; and actually in terms of the gravitation they were built to contend with, it had almost no weight at all.

When the two men returned, they were dressed as were the women, in shorts, and barefoot, with the same transparent gloves. The four of them then began to work together, quickly, expertly—evidently a team who had worked in this manner many times in the past. The mouse now lay upon its stomach, its feet spread. One man put a cone-shaped mask over its head and began the feeding of oxygen. The other man shaved the top of its head with an electric razor, while the two women began an operation which would remove the entire top of the mouse's skull. Working with great speed and skill, they incised the skin, and then using trephines that were armed with a sort of laser beam rather than a saw, they cut through the top of the skull, removed it, and handed it to one of the men who placed it in a pan that was filled with a glowing solution. The brain of the mouse was thus exposed.

The two women then wheeled over a machine with a turret top on a universal joint, lowered the top close to the exposed brain, and pressed a button. About a hundred tiny wires emerged from the turret top, and very fast, the women began to attach these wires to parts of the mouse's brain. The man who had been controlling the oxygen flow now brought over another machine, drew tubes out of it, and began a process of feeding fluid into the mouse's circulatory system, while the second man began to work on the skull section that was in the glowing solution.

The four of them worked steadily and apparently without fatigue. Outside, the night ended and the sun rose, and still the four space people worked on. At about noon they finished the first part of their work and stood back from the table to observe and admire what they had done. The tiny brain of the mouse had been increased fivefold in size, and in shape and folds resembled a miniature human brain. Each of the four shared a feeling of great accomplishment, and they mingled their thoughts and praised each other and then proceeded to complete the operation. The shape of the skull section that had been removed was now compatible with the changed brain, and when they replaced it on the mouse's head, the only noticeable difference in the creature's appearance was a strange, high lump above his eyes. They sealed the breaks and joined the flesh with some sort of plastic, removed the tubes, inserted new tubes, and changed the deep unconsciousness of the mouse to a deep sleep.

For the next five days the mouse slept—but from motionless sleep, its condition changed gradually, until on the fifth day it began to stir and move restlessly, and then on the sixth day it awakened. During these five days it was fed intravenously, massaged constantly, and probed constantly and telepathically. The four space people took turns at entering its mind and feeding it information, and neuron by neuron, section by section, they programmed its newly enlarged brain. They were very skilled at this. They gave the mouse background knowledge, understanding, language, and self-comprehension. They fed it a vast amount of information, balanced the information with a philosophical comprehension of the universe and its meaning, left it as it had been emotionally, without aggression or hostility, but also without fear. When the mouse finally awakened, it knew what it was and how it had become what it was. It still remained a mouse, but in the enchanting wonder and majesty of its mind, it was like no other mouse that had ever lived on the planet Earth.

The four space people stood around the mouse as it awakened and watched it. They were pleased, and since much in their nature, especially in their emotional responses was childlike and direct, they could not help showing their pleasure and smiling at the mouse. Their thoughts were in the nature of a welcome, and all that the mind of the mouse could express was gratitude. The mouse came to its feet, stood on the floor where it had lain, faced each of them in turn, and then wept inwardly at the fact of its existence. Then the mouse was hungry and they gave it food. After that the mouse asked the basic, inevitable question:

"Why?"

"Because we need your help."

"How can I help you when your own wisdom and power are apparently without measure?"

The first spaceman explained. They were explorers, cartographers, surveyors—and behind them, light-years away, was their home planet, a gigantic ball the size of our planet Jupiter. Thus their small size, their incredible density. Weighing on earth only a fraction of what they weighed at home, they nevertheless weighed more than any earth creature their size—so much more that they walked on earth in dire peril of sinking out of sight. It was quite true that they could go anywhere in their spacecraft, but to get all the information they required, they would have to leave it—they would have to venture forth on foot. Thus the mouse would be their eyes and their feet.

"And for this a mouse!" the mouse exclaimed. "Why? I am the smallest, the most defenseless of creatures."

"Not any longer," they assured him. "We ourselves carry no weapons, because we have our minds, and in that way your mind is like ours. You can enter the mind of any creature, a cat, a dog—even a man—stop the neuron paths to his hate and aggression centers, and you can do it with the speed of thought. You have the strongest of all weapons—the ability to make any living thing love you, and having that, you need nothing else."

Thus the mouse became a part of the little group of space people who measured, charted, and examined the planet Earth. The mouse raced through the streets of a hundred cities, slipped in and out of hundreds of buildings, crouched in corners where he was privy to the discussions of people of power who ruled this part or that part of the planet Earth, and the space people listened with his ears, smelled with his sensitive nostrils, and saw with his soft brown eyes. The mouse journeyed thousands of miles, across the seas and continents whose existence he had never dreamed about. He listened to professors lecturing to auditoriums of college students, and he listened to the great symphony orchestras, the fine violinists and pianists. He watched mothers give birth to children and he listened to wars being planned and murders plotted. He saw weeping mourners watch the dead interred in the earth, and he trembled to the crashing sounds of huge assembly lines in monstrous factories. He hugged the earth as bullets whistled overhead, and he saw men slaughter each other for reasons so obscure that in their own minds there was only hate and fear.

As much as the space people, he was a stranger to the curious ways of mankind, and he listened to them speculate on the mindless, haphazard mixture of joy and horror that was mankind's civilization on the planet Earth.

Then, when their mission was almost completed, the mouse chose to ask them about their own place. He was able to weigh facts now and to measure possibilities and to grapple with uncertainties and to create his own abstractions; and so he thought, on one of those evenings when the warmth of the five little creatures filled the spaceship, when they sat and mingled thoughts and reactions in an interlocking of body and mind of which the mouse was a part, about the place where they had been born.

"Is it very beautiful?" the mouse asked.

"It's a good place. Beautiful–and filled with music."

"You have no wars?"

"No."

"And no one kills for the pleasure of killing?"

"No."

"And your animals–things like myself?"

"They exist in their own ecology. We don't disturb it, and we don't kill them. We grow and we make the food we eat."

"And are there crimes like here—murder and assault and robbery?"

"Almost never."

And so it went, question and answer, while the mouse lay there in front of them, his strangely shaped head between his paws, his eyes fixed on the two men and the two women with worship and love; and then it came as he asked them:

"Will I be allowed to live with you—with the four of you? Perhaps to go on other missions with you? Your people are never cruel. You won't place me with the animals. You'll let me be with the people, won't you?"

They didn't answer. The mouse tried to reach into their minds, but he was still like a little child when it came to the game of telepathy, and their minds were shielded.

"Why?"

Still no response.

"Why?" he pleaded.

Then, from one of the women. "We were going to tell you. Not tonight, but soon. Now we must tell you. You can't come with us."

"Why?"

"For the plainest of reasons, dear friend. We are going home."

"Then let me go home with you. It's my home too—the beginning of all my thoughts and dreams and hope."

"We can't."

"Why?" the mouse pleaded. "Why?"

"Don't you understand? Our planet is the size of your planet Jupiter here in the solar system. That is why we were so small in earth terms—because our very atomic structure is different from yours. By the measure of weight they use here on earth, I weigh almost a hundred kilograms, and you weigh less than an eighth of a kilogram, and yet we are almost the same size. If we were to bring you to our planet, you would die the moment we reached its gravitational pull. You would be crushed so completely that all semblance of form in you would disappear. You can't ask us to destroy you."

"But you're so wise," the mouse protested. "You can do almost anything. Change me. Make me like yourselves."

"By your standards we're wise—" The space people were full of sadness. It permeated the room, and the mouse felt its desolation. "By our own standards we have precious little wisdom. We can't make you like us. That is beyond any power we might dream of. We can't even undo what we have done, and now we realize what we have done."

"And what will you do with me?"

"The only thing we can do. Leave you here."

"Oh, no." The thought was a cry of agony.

"What else can we do?"

"Don't leave me here," the mouse begged them. "Anything—but don't leave me here. Let me make the journey with you, and then if I have to die I will die."

"There is no journey as you see it," they explained. "Space is not an area for us. We can't make it comprehensible to you, only to tell you that it is an illusion. When we rise out of the earth's atmosphere, we slip into a fold of space and emerge in our own planetary system. So it would not be a journey that you would make with us—only a step to your death."

"Then let me die with you," the mouse pleaded.

"No—you ask us to kill you. We can't."

"Yet you made me."

"We changed you. We made you grow in a certain way."

"Did I ask you to? Did you ask me whether I wanted to be like this?"

"God help us, we didn't."

"Then what am I to do?"

"Live. That's all we can say. You must live."

"How? How can I live? A mouse hides in the grass and knows only two things—fear and hunger. It doesn't even know that it is, and of the vast lunatic world that surrounds it, it knows nothing. But you gave me the knowledge—"

"And we also gave you the means to defend yourself, so that you can live without fear."

"Why? Why should I live? Don't you understand that?"

"Because life is good and beautiful—and in itself the answer to all things."

"For me?" The mouse looked at them and begged them to look at him. "What do you see? I am a mouse. In all this world there is no other creature like myself. Shall I go back to the mice?"

"Perhaps."

"And discuss philosophy with them? And open my mind to them? Or should I have intercourse with those poor, damned mindless creatures? What am I to do? You are wise. Tell me. Shall I be the stallion of the mouse world? Shall I store up riches in roots and bulbs? Tell me, tell me," he pleaded.

"We will talk about it again," the space people said. "Be with yourself for a while, and don't be afraid."

Then the mouse lay with his head between his paws and he thought about the way things were. And when the space people asked him where he wanted to be, he told them:

"Where you found me."

So once again the saucer settled by night into the back yard of the surburban split-level house. Once again the air lock opened, and this time a mouse emerged. The mouse stood there, and the saucer rose out of the swirling dead leaves and spun away, a fleck of gold losing itself in the night. And the mouse stood there, facing its own eternity.

A cat, awakened by the movement among the leaves, came toward the mouse and then halted a few inches away when the tiny animal did not flee. The cat reached out a paw, and then the paw stopped. The cat struggled for control of its own body and then it fled, and still the mouse stood motionless. Then the mouse smelled the air, oriented himself, and moved to the mouth of an old mole tunnel. From down below, from deep in the tunnel, came the warm, musky odor of mice. The mouse went down through the tunnel to the nest, where a male and a female mouse crouched, and the mouse probed into their minds and found fear and hunger.

The mouse ran from the tunnel up to the open air and stood there, sobbing and panting. He turned his head up to the sky and reached out with his mind—but what he tried to reach was already a hundred light-years away.

"Why? Why?" the mouse sobbed to himself. "They are so good, so wise—why did they do it to me?"

He then moved toward the house. He had become an adept at entering houses, and only a steel vault would have defied him. He found his point of entry and slipped into the cellar of the house. His night vision was good, and this combined with his keen sense of smell enabled him to move swiftly and at will.

Moving through the shifting web of strong odors that marked any habitation of people, he isolated the sharp smell of old cheese, and he moved across the floor and under a staircase to where a mousetrap had been set. It was a primitive thing, a stirrup of hard wire bent back against the tension of a coil spring and held with a tiny latch. The bit of cheese was on the latch, and the lightest touch on the cheese would spring the trap.

Filled with pity for his own kind, their gentleness, their helplessness, their mindless hunger that led them into a trap so simple and unconcealed, the mouse felt a sudden sense of triumph, of ultimate knowledge. He knew now what the space people had known from the very beginning, that they had given him the ultimate gift of the universe—consciousness of his own being—and in the flash of that knowledge the mouse knew all things and knew that all things were encompassed in consciousness. He saw the wholeness of the world and of all the worlds that ever were or would be, and he was without fear or loneliness.

IN THE MORNING, the man of the split-level suburban house went down into his cellar and let out a whoop of delight.

"Got it," he yelled up to his family. "I got the little bastard now."

But the man never really looked at anything, not at his wife, not at his kids, not at the world; and while he knew that the trap contained a dead mouse, he never even noticed that this mouse was somewhat different from the other mice. Instead, he went out to the back yard, swung the dead mouse by his tail, and sent it flying into his neighbor's back yard.

"That'll give him something to think about," the man said, grinning.

the vision of milty boil

Napoleon, Stalin, Hitler, and Mussolini all had one thing in common with Milton Boil: they were short men. But the most explosive moments in human history have often been the result of an absent six or seven inches in height, and while it is hardly profitable it is certainly interesting to speculate upon what might have been man's destiny had Milton Boil been six feet and one inch instead of five feet and one inch—with a name like Smith or Jones or Goldberg instead of Boil.

But at his maturity he was five feet and one inch, and his name had already caused him so much small suffering that no force on earth would have persuaded him to change it. All his life he had been stuck with pins, pinched and punned upon because of his name and his height; no wonder he was a millionaire before he reached thirty.

He was born in 1940 and he grew up in the time of affluence. His father was a builder of small apartment houses. Milton (or Milty, as he came to be known the world over) came out of college, spent a year learning more about his father's business than the old man ever knew, and then parted company with his father and built his first big apartment house. Milty was a genius. By 1970 he had become the largest builder of apartment houses in New York City. He married Joan Pebbleman, whose father was one of the country's largest builders of office buildings, and they had three lovely children. Joan worked in charitable efforts. Her name was in *The New York Times* at least once a week. She was only four feet and ten inches tall, so from a reasonable distance they were a very handsome couple indeed.

Milty respected money, rich people, brains, organizational drive, very rich people, the government, the church, and millionaires. In an interview, he was asked what he considered the first necessary attribute of a young man who desired to become a millionaire.

"Ambition," he replied promptly. He respected ambition.

"And after that?"

"Influence," he replied. "Proper friends."

And Milty made friends and built influence. By 1975, at the age of thirty-five, he was considered the most influential man in New York City. His influence was such that he was able to have a number of significant changes made in the building code—among them the lowering of the minimum height of the ceilings to seven feet. With this achieved, he built the first one-hundred-story apartment house in New York. In 1980, riding the crest of the wave created by the population explosion, Milty Boil managed to have the city council pass an ordinance permitting ceilings of six feet in all apartment buildings over fifty stories high.

Rival builders sneered at Milty's new house, claiming that no one would be so damn foolish as to rent an apartment with six-foot ceilings, but such was the housing shortage by then that the entire building, with its seven hundred apartments, was fully rented in sixty days.

The cash flow that passed through Milty's deserving hands had by now become so enormous that he was known throughout the business as the "golden boy" or, more often, "the golden boil"; but Milty was beyond the barbs of name-calling. His vision and imagination had lifted him to unprecedented heights, and once again he brought his influence to bear upon the lawmakers. In 1982 his workmen broke ground for a new building of one hundred stories, with ceilings five feet high. Biographers recall this as a moment of great crisis in the life of Milty Boil, and historians look back upon it as a turning point in man's destiny. Suddenly all the forces of conservatism focused upon Milty; he was called everything from a depraved profiteer to public enemy number one; he was abused in the press, in Congress, on the air. There were, of course, a handful of farsighted people who applauded Milty's courage and creativity, but mostly it was abuse that he received. And to this, at his now historic press conference, Milty replied simply and with dignity:

"I give people a place to live at a reasonable rent. Especially the young people, who so desperately desire an urban condition. I give them a place to live at a rent they can afford."

"Do you, sir?" demanded the representative of *The New York Times*, bold and caustic as befitting his place, leading the attack upon Milty. "How can you say that in the light of the fact that we Americans are the tallest people on earth, especially our youth?"

"I agree," Milty replied. "This height is a tribute to the

American way of life. All my life I have upheld the American way of life."

"That hardly answers the question," said a CBS man.

"I intend to answer it," Milty assured them. "I have never been less than forthright about my plans. I have submitted this problem to a panel of forty-two physicians. They all agree that bending, crouching, and occasional creeping can only be beneficial to human health. Thereby a whole series of muscles formerly ignored are brought into play, and thus my own efforts coincide with the President's plan for physical fitness. As for the defense of democracy on an international scale, nothing better develops a man for jungle combat than the alertness produced by life in a five-foot-high apartment. I have here a statement from the Secretary of Defense—mimeographed copies available—which says in part: 'The constant concerns for his country's welfare which dominate the thinking of Milton Boil deserve special mention and commendation.' I also have statements from Generals Bosch and Korpulant, both of them experts—"

"Mr. Boil," he was interrupted, "are you trying to tell us that these low ceilings constitute a positive, progressive feature in apartment construction?"

"They do indeed. Furthermore, an apartment is not a place where one lives vertically. We have conducted a survey of the habits of over ten thousand apartment dwellers, and the results show that ninety-two point eight percent of their hours spent in the apartment are spent in a sitting or reclining or prone position. With young married couples, the percentage is a trifle higher—"

So did Milty Boil defend himself, a man alone fighting off

the forces of reaction and always contemplating the gigantic profit produced by a building consisting of five-foot-high apartments. But a day later, at his regular board of directors' meeting, Milty found that even those who shared the profits had their doubts.

"It won't work."

"Milty—you can't go on this way. I hear Washington intends to step in."

"Did you hear what *Pravda* has to say? I have the translation here—'the final step in the decadence of the United States.' Well, it gives one pause."

"I don't say it wasn't a brilliant step, Milty. I simply ask: Will it work? Can it work? *Life* is not *Pravda*, but listen to its editorial: 'Has Milty finally flipped? We don't hold with those who characterize Milton Boil as a madman or public enemy. We recognize that the greatest builder of modern America does not make decisions lightly. But if Milton Boil is not mad, neither are Americans three feet tall. If—'"

"No, no!" Milty cried, finally coming to life in his place at the head of the table. "Hold it right there. Read that last sentence again."

"What last sentence?"

"You know—that business about three feet tall."

"You mean this—'But if Milton Boil is not mad, neither are Americans three feet tall—'"

"Right! Right you are! There it is!"

"There what is?" asked one of the older members, less able because of his age to follow the pyrotechnics of Milty's thought.

"The whole thing. The whole answer. The key to everything." Milty's very real excitement began to permeate the others.

"What key, Milty? Don't be so damned mysterious."

"All right. But tell me this. What is the number one problem of the world today?"

"Communism," half a dozen board members replied eagerly.

"Nuts! Communism is a word. We licked them in space and we licked them in everything else down here. Our houses are better and our roads are better and our factories are better."

"Disease," someone said hopefully.

"Did you ever hear of antibiotics? Not disease."

"War, Milty?"

"Since when is war a problem?"

"Inflation?"

"You should talk—you made millions out of inflation. Come on, come on, use your heads—there's only one number one problem in the world today, and if we lick it, it licks us, and if we destroy it, it destroys us—until now, until right this minute when your uncle Milty Boil solved it, and we're going to lick it and it's not going to destroy us."

They spread their hands hopelessly. They looked at Milty in defeat, knowing how much he enjoyed winning.

"Milty, let us in, tell us where the action is," his first vice-president pleaded.

"All right." Milty Boil leaned forward. His face hardened; his voice became precise and crisp. He was all mind now, a cold, beautiful, hard-core calculating machine. They knew that look on Milty's face; they knew it meant a breakthrough, action, action, and more action. The silence at the board table became a thing in itself.

"All right. World's number one problem—overpopulation, namely the population explosion. Next—what is our market for anything. People. And how do you increase a market? More people. But with more people you got the population explosion. Mankind trapped. Finis. Over. The earth starves."

"Right, Milty," the board whispered.

"But there's a way."

The board waited.

Slowly, measuring each word, Milty said, "Double the size of the earth. That's the solution. That takes care of the next hundred years."

The members of the board relaxed, looked at each other, grinned, and then burst into laughter. Only Milty didn't laugh. His face stony-set and cold as ice, he regarded them without pleasure and waited. They saw his expression finally, and the laughter died away. Milty pointed one finger at his second vice-president, who was in charge of purchasing, and asked evenly:

"Just what in hell do you find so funny?"

"The jest, Milty. We're laughing with you."

"Why?"

"Because it's a yuk, Milty, a tribute, so as to speak. You got a sense of humor like nobody else."

"I don't think it's funny," Milty said.

"No? But you got to be kidding, Milty. The earth is what it is. Twenty-five thousand miles in circumference. That's fourth-grade stuff."

"And you got a fourth-grade mind."

"Milty, Milty," said the oldest member in a fatherly way, "Milty, you have a fine mind, but nobody makes the earth larger."

"No?"

"No, Milty, I am afraid not."

"All right," Milty said, unperturbed by the oldest member and smiling slightly. "Nobody makes the earth larger. But tell me this—suppose, just for the sake of argument, that the average man was three feet tall. Now if he kept the same scale in relation to himself, everything would be reduced by half. Six inches would be a foot, and a mile would become two miles. In other words, if the man is reduced in size to one-half, then so are all his measurements. Suddenly the world is not twenty-five thousand miles in circumference but fifty thousand miles in circumference. We have doubled the size of the earth."

"Milty, Milty," said the oldest member, still in a fatherly way, "Milty, you got a brain like a steel trap. But all you are actually doing is to buttress one impossible statement with another. To make men three feet tall is as impossible as to make the earth fifty thousand miles in diameter."

"Who says?"

"I say, Milty," continued the oldest member. "I was a friend of your father, may he rest in peace, so I have the right."

"Good," Milty said. "You got the right. Now shut up." And to the rest of the board:

"I say we can produce the three-foot man."

"How, Milty?" asked the youngest member of the board. He was with Milty all the way.

"How? First I ask this: what in hell is so great about tall? Tall, tall, tall—that's all you hear. Why? Was Adolf Hitler tall? Was Napoleon tall? Was Onassis tall? Was Willie Shoemaker tall? And do you know how much prize money he took? Over thirty million, that's all. How about art—was Toulouse-Lautrec tall?

You know how tall they believe Shakespeare was? Five feet four inches. Tall is for basketball players."

"But people think tall, Milty."

"Then we change their thinking. They think tall because everywhere the propaganda says that tall is good. We change that. We show them that tall is for clods. The men who make the world go round are small. The men women prefer are small. The men who become top dog are small. It's a small man's world. That's what we show the world—that it's a small man's world, and the smaller the better."

"But, Milty," the oldest member of the board said patiently, "suppose we demonstrate all that. We still can't make men smaller."

"No?" Milty smiled. Years later, remembering that smile, some of the younger board members spoke about a "Gioconda" quality, but that was in retrospect and after Milty had gone to whatever rewards the next world provides for such genius. At the moment, then in 1982, Milty's smile was a smile of sheer superior knowledge.

"No—no, we can't make men smaller, but they can, can't they?"

"How, Milty?"

"By wanting it. Men have increased their height by over a foot in the past two hundred years. Suppose they start to decrease it—"

A month later, in the same board room, facing the representatives of the twelve largest advertising agencies in the world and the seventeen largest public relations firms, Milty Boil put his plan on its proper level.

"We are here, ladies and gentlemen," he said, "to serve mankind. In the name of mankind, its purpose and its survival, I call this meeting to order. Our goal, my friends, is to double the size of the earth."

Then, to the silent—silent, that is, until he had finished—admiration of those assembled there, Milty presented his plan; and then even those hard-bitten, cynical representatives of the one business that makes the earth turn broke into cheers and applause. Milty rose and nodded modestly; he was not egotistical, but neither was he one to hide his light under a bushel.

"Thank you," he said quietly. "And now the floor is open for ideas and questions."

No stodgy board of directors were these twenty-nine representatives of advertising and public relations. Their minds were as hard and bright as quartz. The first to rise was Jack Aberdeen, the young wonder boy of Carrol, Carrol, Carrol and Quince. Even as he snapped his fingers, Milty could see his mind crackle and snap.

"Got it, Mr. Boil. Round number one. You know the way the Kellogg Company pushes its cornflakes account. I see a new competitive product. *Tinies.* I got the slogan—'Small and tight.' Every company will have to fall in line. 'Are you afraid of the big bully? *Tinies* will reduce your muscles to knots of steel. Tiny knots of steel. Small and tight.' I got a tune for it—'Small and tight, small and tight, who the hell needs height, if only I am small and tight?' Of course we got to find something like an anti-vitamin, but we represent Associated Labs, and I'll get to work on it."

Milty could have hugged the kid, but already Steve Johnson of Kelly, Cohen and Clark was on his feet and speaking. He represented some of the biggest airlines on earth.

"Milty," he said, "may we call you Milty?"

"Call me Milty, Steve. By all means."

"Two things. Milty, you have just kicked off the biggest change in the history of airlines. That's number one. I got the slogan—'Weigh less, pay less.' Why not? The small man weighs less, he pays less. Put a premium on small."

Johnson, Milty noted, was no taller than he himself.

"Second thing—flights to the moon and Mars. All the airlines have been discussing the prospect of putting these flights on a tourist basis. But the cost is terrifying. We make it a bonus thing: 'Do you want to see the moon? You can't—you're too tall. But your kids can. Keep them small. Feed them anti-vitamins. So that they may have what you never dreamed of having—a flight to the moon or Mars—a step into tomorrow, a glimpse of man's glorious future. No tourist who is taller than five feet can get into outer space.' How about that—is it not beautiful?"

Cathey Brodie, public relations for Jones and Keppleman, the largest ethical drug house in the world, leaped to her feet now and cried out:

"Moon pills—does that ever send me! It means the lab boys have to really dig for something to control height, but they've found everything else. Why not? Moon pills."

"Moon pills," Milty repeated, smiling.

Tab Henderson, who managed promotion for over eight hundred large hospitals, not to mention three of the leading insurance companies, jumped right into the gap Cathey Brodie had opened.

"We could just overlook the biggest little inducement in this whole splendid project. I mean health. Long life. Added years. We have statistical charts to show that over six feet three inches, life expectancy begins to decrease. We look at it the other way. Be small and stay healthy."

There were a few sour faces, a few spoil-sports, but most of the team assembled threw their hats into the ring, and the plans came thick and fast.

"Tall, dark, and handsome—that must go. Small for tall—'Small, dark, and handsome.'"

"Beautiful."

"Get the sex angle. 'Sex is better with a small man or a small woman.'"

"'Try it with both—make your own decision.' That gives it a do-it-yourself feeling."

"How about this—'Close the generation gap!' For the past three or four generations the kids have all been bigger than their parents. No wonder a father can't lay down the law. Now we reverse it, each generation smaller than the one that preceded it. We reestablish the authority of the father. The home once again becomes the sanctuary it was in olden times."

One after another the ideas sparked forth, until the beginnings of an entire world program began to take shape there in the board room of Boil Enterprises. Rome wasn't built in a day, and neither was the pattern of world psychology that reduced practically all of the human race to half of its size; but there the foundation was laid—and there Milty Boil became Milty Boil, benefactor, underwriting that first, initial effort with a cool twenty million dollars of his own money.

For the rest of his life Milty had a goal—a reason and a meaning for the tremendous effort that produced one of the great fortunes of our time. Cynical people say that the first five years of the program created a condition where Milty Boil could begin to build his gigantic structures—one hundred floors with ceilings only four feet and six inches high—without opposition. Others—so-called reformers—held that it was an indignity for man to spend his life in a place where he could never hope to stand up straight, but Milty answered that charge with his ringing Declaration of Purpose, a document which takes it place in American history alongside the Declaration of Independence and the Gettysburg Address. I quote only the first paragraph of Milty's Declaration, for I am sure that most of my readers know it by heart.

"Life without purpose," wrote Milty (or some unknown ghost writer who took his inspiration from the dynamic leadership of Milton Boil), "is neither life nor death but a dull and wretched existence unworthy of man. Man must have a goal, a purpose, a destination, a shining goal for which he struggles. We saw in the hapless youth of the sixties and seventies what it meant to be without a purpose in life; but never again shall the world face that quandary. People—shameless people—have accused me of building for profit; they charge that I reduce man with my low ceilings, that I take away his dignity. But the reverse is true. Through my splendid houses, man has found both dignity and purpose—the purpose to be small and to raise small children, so that the world may increase in size, and the dignity of men who must always fight their environment, who cannot stand in decadent comfort, who must struggle and grow through struggle."

In the year 2010, when Milty was seventy years old, he achieved his ultimate goal. Through his ever expanding influence, he persuaded the New York City Council to pass a law cutting Central Park in half, granting all that part of it north of Eighty-second Street and south of Ninety-eighth Street to Milton Boil, so that he might fulfill his lifelong dream and build an apartment house two hundred stories tall with ceilings three feet and six inches high. Over a hundred people were killed in the riots that followed this action of the City Council, but progress is never achieved without paying a price, and Milty saw to it that no widow or child of those who had perished went hungry. Also, he guaranteed living space in his new building to all those made fatherless by the riots—at one-half the rent paid by the regular tenants.

After that, only fanatics and hippies would deny that Milty was the gentlest and kindest of landlords in all the history of landlordism. Indeed, after his death, the Pope instituted proceedings that would result in Milty's eventually becoming the patron saint of all landlords; but this is still in the future—with many thorns strewn on the path to sainthood, not to mention certain confusion about Milty's religion, that is, considering that he had any.

Milty died in his eighty-seventh year, and we can be pleased that he lived long enough to see his dream begin to come to fruition. His coffin was carried by eight young men, no one of them more than four feet eight inches in height, and here and there in the audience that packed the chapel were grown men and women no taller than four feet. Of course, these were the exceptions, and it was not until almost half a century later that the first generation of adults who were less than three feet tall reached their maturity.

But we must not abandon this small tribute without noting that when Milty's will was read, it disposed of no more than a few thousand dollars and a handful of things that were beloved of him. Such was the nature of the man who earned millions only to give them away. Naturally, there are those who claim that since reading a book in his very early youth, titled *How to Avoid Probate*, Milty was never subsequently without it—that is, without this precious volume—and that eventually he memorized all of its contents and could quote chapter and verse at will.

But where is there a great man who has not suffered the barbs of envy and hatred? Slander is the burden the great must carry, and Milton Boil carried it as silently and patiently as any man.

On the modest headstone that graces his final resting place, an epitaph written by Milty himself is carved:

"He found them tall and left them small."

To which our generation, standing erect and proud under our three-foot ceilings, can only add a grateful amen.

the mohawk

When Clyde Lightfeather walked up the steps of St. Patrick's Cathedral on Fifth Avenue, he was wearing an old raincoat of sorts; and then he took it off and sat down cross-legged in front of the great doors. Underneath he was dressed just like the bang-bang man in an old Indian medicine show—that is, he wore soft doeskin leggings, woods moccasins, and nothing at all from the waist up. His hair was cut in the traditional central brush style of the scalp lock, with one white feather through the little braid at the back of his neck. He was altogether a very well-built and prepossessing young full-blooded Mohawk Indian.

A crowd gathered because it doesn't take anything very much to gather a crowd in New York, and Father Michael O'Conner came out of the cathedral and Officer Patrick Muldoon came up from the street, and the gentle June sun shone down upon everyone.

"Now just what the hell are you up to?" Officer Muldoon asked Clyde Lightfeather. There was a querulous note in Officer Muldoon's voice, for he was sick and tired of freaks, hard-core hippies, acid-heads, pot-heads, love children and flower children, black power folk, SDS, sit-ins and demonstrations-out; and while he was fond of saying that he had seen everything, he had never before seen a Mohawk Indian sitting cross-legged in front of St. Patrick's.

"God and God's grace, I suppose," Clyde Lightfeather answered.

"Now don't you know," said Muldoon, his voice taking that tired, descending path of patience and veiled threat, "that this is private property and that you cannot put a feather in your hair and just sit yourself down and attract a crowd and make difficulties for honest worshipers?"

"Why not? This isn't private property. This is God's property, and since you don't work for God, why don't you take your big, fat blue ass out of here and leave me alone?"

Officer Muldoon began to make the proper response to such talk, Mohawk Indian or not—with the crowd grinning and half disposed toward the Indian—when Father O'Conner intervened and pointed out to Officer Muldoon that the Indian was absolutely right. This was not private property but God's property.

"The devil you say!" Officer Muldoon exclaimed. "You're going to let that heathen sit there?"

Up until that moment Father O'Conner had been of a mind to say a few reasonable words that would be persuasive enough to move the Indian away. Now he abruptly changed his position.

"Maybe I will," he declared.

"Thank you," Lightfeather said.

"Providing you give me one good reason why I should."

"Because I am here to meditate."

"And you consider this a proper place for meditation, Mr.—?"

"Lightfeather."

"Mr. Lightfeather."

"The best. Do you deny that?" he demanded pugnaciously.

"What is meditation to you, Mr. Lightfeather?"

"Prayer—God—being."

"Then how can I deny it?" the priest asked.

"And you're going to let him stay there?" Muldoon demanded.

"I think so."

"Now look," Muldoon said, "I was raised a Catholic, and maybe I don't know much, but I know one thing—a cathedral is made for worship on the inside, not on the outside!"

Nevertheless, the Indian remained there, and within a few hours the television cameras and the newspapermen were there and Father O'Conner was facing no less exalted a person than the Cardinal himself. The research facilities at the various networks were concentrated upon the letter *m*—*m* for meditation as well as Mohawk. Chet Huntley informed millions, not only that meditation was a significant, inwardly directed spiritual exercise, an inner concentration upon some thought of deep religious significance, but that the Mohawk Indians had been great in their time, the organizing force of the mighty Six Nations of the Iroquois Confederacy. The peace of the forests was the Mohawk peace, even as the law was the Mohawk law, codified in ancient times by that gentle and wise man, Hiawatha. From the St. Lawrence River in the north to the Hudson River in the south, the Mohawk peace and the Mohawk law prevailed before the white man's coming.

Less historically oriented, the CBS commentators wondered whether this was not simply another bit of hooliganism inflicted by college youth upon a patient public. They had researched Lightfeather himself, learning that, after Harvard, he took his Ph.D. at Columbia—his doctoral paper being a study of the use of various hallucinogenic plants in American Indian religions. "It is discouraging," said Walter Cronkite, "to find a young American Indian of such brilliance engaging in such tiresome antics."

His Eminence, the Cardinal, took another tack entirely. It was not his to unravel a Mohawk Indian. Instead he coldly asked Father O'Conner just what he proposed.

"Well, sir, Your Eminence, I mean he's not doing any harm, is he?"

"Really carried away by the notion that God owns the property—am I right, Father?"

"Well—he put it so naturally and directly, Your Eminence."

"Did it ever occur to you that God's property rights extend even farther than St. Patrick's? You know He owns Wall Street and the White House and Protestant churches and quite a few synagogues and the Soviet Union and even Red China, not to mention a galaxy or two out there. So if I were you, Father O'Conner, I would suggest some more suitable place than the porch of St. Patrick's for meditation. I would say that you should persuade him to leave by morning."

"Yes, Your Eminence."

"Peacefully."

"Yes, Your Eminence."

"We have still not had a sit-down in St. Patrick's."

"I understand perfectly, Your Eminence."

But Father O'Conner's plan of action was a little less than

perfect. It was about five o'clock in the afternoon now, and the streets were filled with people hurrying home. As little as it takes to make a crowd in New York, it takes less to dispel it; and by now the Indian was wholly taken for granted. Father O'Conner stood next to Lightfeather for a while, brooding as creatively as he could, and then asked politely whether the Indian heard him.

"Why not? Meditation is a condition of alertness, not of sleep."

"You were very still."

"Inside, Father, I am still."

"Why did you come here?" Father O'Conner asked.

"I told you why. To meditate."

"Why here?"

"Because the vibes are good here."

"Vibes?"

"Vibrations."

"Oh."

"It's a question of belief. This place is filled with belief. That's why I picked it. I need belief."

"For what?" Father O'Conner asked curiously.

"So I can believe."

"What do you want to believe?"

"That God is sane."

"I assure you—He is," Father O'Conner said with conviction.

"How the hell do you know?"

"It's a matter of my own belief."

"Not if you were a Mohawk Indian."

"I don't know. I have never been a Mohawk Indian."

"I have."

Father O'Conner thought about it for a moment or two, and in all fairness he could not deny that a Mohawk Indian might have quite a different point of view.

"His Eminence, the Cardinal, is provoked at me," he said finally. "He wants me to persuade you to leave."

"So you're bringing back the fuzz."

"No, peacefully."

"Before you were with me on this being God's pad. Has His Eminence talked you out of that?"

"He pointed out that the Almighty has equal claim to the Soviet Union. I suppose wherever it is, the tenants make the rules."

"All right. Spell it out."

"I hate to be a top sergeant about it," Father O'Conner said. "How long were you planning to stay?"

"Until God answers me."

"That can be a long time," Father O'Conner said unhappily.

"Or an instant. I am meditating on time."

"Time?"

"I always think of time when I think of God," the Indian said. "He has His time. We have ours. I want Him to open His time to me. What in hell am I doing here on Fifth Avenue? I'm a Mohawk Indian. Right?"

Father O'Conner nodded.

"I don't know," the Indian said. "We'll give it the old school try, and then you can call the fuzz. How about it? Until morning?"

"Until morning," Father O'Conner said.

"I'll do as much for you sometime," the Indian said, and those were the last words he was heard to say. The newspaper reporters came down and the television crowd made a second visit, but the Indian was through talking.

The Indian was meditating. He allowed thought to leave his mind and he watched his breath go in and out and he became a sort of a universe unto himself. He considered God's time and he considered man's time–but without thought. There are no thoughts known to man that are capable of dealing even with man's time, much less God's time; but the Indian was not so far from his ancestors as to be trapped in thought. His ancestors had known the secret of the *great time*, which all white men have forgotten.

The Indian was photographed and televised until even the networks had enough of him, and Father O'Conner remained there to see that the Indian's meditation was not interrupted. The priest felt a great kinship with the Indian, but being a priest, he also knew how many had asked and how few had been answered.

By midnight the press had gone and even the few passers-by ignored the Indian. Father O'Conner was amazed at how long he had remained there, motionless, in what is called the lotus position, but he had always heard that Indians were stoical and enduring of pain and desire and he supposed that this Indian was no different. The priest was gratified that the June night was so warm and pleasant; at least the Indian would not suffer from the cold.

Before the priest fell asleep that night, he prayed that some sort of grace might be bestowed upon the Indian. What kind of grace he wasn't at all sure, nor was he ready to plead that the Indian should have a taste of God's time. The notion of God's time was just a bit terrifying to Father O'Conner.

He slept well but not for long, and he was up and dressed with the first gray presence of dawn. The priest walked to the porch of the cathedral, and there was the Indian exactly as the priest had left him. So erect, so unmoving was his body that, were it not for the slight motion of his bare stomach, the priest might have thought him dead.

As for the Indian, Clyde Lightfeather, he was alert and within himself, and his mind was clear and open. Eyes closed, he felt the breezes of dawn on his cheek, the scent of morning in his nostril. He had no need for prayer; his whole being was a gentle reminder; and that way he heard a bird singing.

He allowed the sound to pass through him; he experienced it but did not detain it. And then he heard the leaping, gurgling passage of a brook. That too he heard without detention. And then he smelled the smell of the earth in June, the wonderful wet, sweet, thick smell of life coming and life going, and this smell he clung to, for he knew that his meditation was finished and that he had been granted a moment of God's time.

He opened his eyes, and instead of the great masses of Rockefeller Center, he saw an ancient stand of tulip trees, each of them fifteen feet across the base and reaching so high up that only the birds knew where they topped out. Thin fingers of the dawn laced through the tulips, and out of the great knowledge that comes with the great time, the Indian knew that there would be birch-bark canoes on the shore of the Hudson, carefully sheltered for the day they would be needed, and that the Hudson was the road to the Mohawk Valley where the longhouses stood. He waited no longer but leaped to his feet and raced through the tulip trees.

The priest had turned for a moment to regard the soaring

majesty of St. Patrick's; when he looked again, the Indian was gone. Instead of being pleased that he had accomplished what the Cardinal desired, the priest felt a sense of loss.

A few hours later the Cardinal sent for Father O'Conner, and the priest told him that the Indian had left very early in the morning.

"There was no unpleasantness, I trust?"

"No, Your Eminence."

"No police?"

"No, sir—only myself." Father O'Conner hesitated, swallowed, and instead of departing, coughed.

"Yes?" the Cardinal asked.

"If I may ask you a question, Your Eminence?"

"Go ahead."

"What is God's time, Your Eminence?"

The Cardinal smiled, but not with amusement. The smile was a turning inward, as if he were remembering things that had happened long, long ago.

"Was that the Indian's notion?"

Father O'Conner nodded with embarrassment.

"Did you ask him?"

"No, I did not."

"Then when he returns," the Cardinal said, "I suggest that you do."

the wound

Max Gaffey always insisted that the essence of the oil industry could be summed up in a simple statement: the right thing in the wrong place. My wife, Martha, always disliked him and said that he was a spoiler. I suppose he was, but how was he different from any of us in that sense? We were all spoilers, and if we were not the actual thing, we invested in it and thereby became rich. I myself had invested the small nest egg that a college professor puts away in a stock Max Gaffey gave me. It was called Thunder Inc., and the company's function was to use atomic bombs to release natural gas and oil locked up in the vast untouched shale deposits that we have here in the United States.

Oil shale is not a very economical source of oil. The oil is locked up in the shale, and about 60 percent of the total cost of shale oil consists of the laborious methods of mining the shale, crushing it to release the oil, and then disposing of the spent shale.

Gaffey sold to Thunder Inc. an entirely new method, which involved the use of surplus atomic bombs for the release of shale oil. In very simplistic terms, a deep hole is bored in shale-oil deposits. Then an atomic bomb is lowered to the bottom of this hole, after which the hole is plugged and the bomb is detonated. Theoretically, the heat and force of the atomic explosion crushes the shale and releases the oil to fill the underground cavern formed by the gigantic force of the bomb. The oil does not burn because the hole is sealed, and thereby, for a comparatively small cost, untold amounts of oil can be tapped and released—enough perhaps to last until that time when we experience a complete conversion to atomic energy—so vast are the shale deposits.

Such at least was the way Max Gaffey put the proposition to me, in a sort of mutual brain-picking operation. He had the utmost admiration for my knowledge of the earth's crust, and I had an equally profound admiration for his ability to make two or five or ten dollars appear where only one had been before.

My wife disliked him and his notions, and most of all the proposal to feed atomic bombs into the earth's crust.

"It's wrong," she said flatly. "I don't know why or how, but this I do know, that everything connected with that wretched bomb is wrong."

"Yet couldn't you look at this as a sort of salvation?" I argued. "Here we are in these United States with enough atom bombs to destroy life on ten earths the size of ours—and every one of those bombs represents an investment of millions of dollars. I could not agree more when you hold that those bombs are the most hideous and frightful things the mind of man ever conceived."

"Then how on earth can you speak of salvation?"

"Because so long as those bombs sit here, they represent a

constant threat—day and night the threat that some feather-brained general or brainless politician will begin the process of throwing them at our neighbors. But here Gaffey has come up with a peaceful use for the bomb. Don't you see what that means?"

"I'm afraid I don't," Martha said.

"It means that we can use the damn bombs for something other than suicide—because if this starts, it's the end of mankind. But there are oil-shale and gas-shale deposits all over the earth, and if we can use the bomb to supply man with a century of fuel, not to mention the chemical by-products, we may just find a way to dispose of those filthy bombs."

"Oh, you don't believe that for a moment," Martha snorted.

"I do. I certainly do."

And I think I did. I went over the plans that Gaffey and his associates had worked out, and I could not find any flaw. If the hole were plugged properly, there would be no fallout. We knew that and we had the know-how to plug the hole, and we had proven it in at least twenty underground explosions. The earth tremor would be inconsequential; in spite of the heat, the oil would not ignite, and in spite of the cost of the atom bombs, the savings would be monumental. In fact, Gaffey hinted that some accommodation between the government and Thunder Inc. was in the process of being worked out, and if it went through as planned, the atom bombs might just cost Thunder Inc. nothing at all, the whole thing being in the way of an experiment for the social good.

After all, Thunder Inc. did not own any oil-shale deposits, nor was it in the oil business. It was simply a service organization with the proper know-how and for a fee—if the process worked—it would release the oil for others. What the fee would be was left unsaid, but Max Gaffey, in return for my consultation, suggested that I might buy a few shares, not only of Thunder Inc., but of General Shale Holdings.

I had altogether about ten thousand dollars in savings available and another ten thousand in American Telephone and government bonds. Martha had a bit of money of her own, but I left that alone, and without telling her, I sold my Telephone stock and my bonds. Thunder Inc. was selling at five dollars a share, and I bought two thousand shares. General Shale was selling for two dollars, and I bought four thousand shares. I saw nothing immoral—as business morality was calculated—in the procedures adopted by Thunder Inc. Its relationship to the government was no different than the relationships of various other companies, and my own process of investment was perfectly straightforward and honorable. I was not even the recipient of secret information, for the atom-bomb-shale-oil proposal had been widely publicized if little believed.

Even before the first test explosion was undertaken, the stock of Thunder Inc. went from five to sixty-five dollars a share. My ten thousand dollars became one hundred and thirty thousand, and that doubled again a year later. The four thousand shares of General Shale went up to eighteen dollars a share; and from a moderately poor professor I became a moderately rich professor. When finally, almost two years after Max Gaffey first approached me, they exploded the first atom bomb in a shaft reamed in the oil-shale deposits, I had abandoned the simple anxieties of the poor and had developed an entirely new set tailored for the upper middle class. We became a two-car family, and a reluctant Martha joined me in shopping for a larger house. In the new house, Gaffey and his wife came to dinner, and Martha armed herself with two stiff martinis. Then she was quietly polite until Gaffey began to talk about the social good. He painted a bright picture of what shale oil could do and how rich we might well become.

"Oh, yes—yes," Martha agreed. "Polute the atmosphere, kill more people with more cars, increase the speed with which we can buzz around in circles and get precisely nowhere."

"Oh, you're a pessimist," said Gaffey's wife, who was young and pretty but no mental giant.

"Of course there are two sides to it," Gaffey admitted. "It's a question of controls. You can't stop progress, but it seems to me that you can direct it."

"The way we've been directing it—so that our rivers stink and our lakes are sewers of dead fish and our atmosphere is polluted and our birds are poisoned by DDT and our natural resources are spoiled. We are all spoilers, aren't we?"

"Come now," I protested, "this is the way it is, and all of us are indignant about it, Martha."

"Are you, really?"

"I think so."

"Men have always dug in the earth," Gaffey said. "Otherwise we'd still be in the Stone Age."

"And perhaps a good bit happier."

"No, no, no," I said. "The Stone Age was a very unpleasant time, Martha. You don't wish us back there."

"Do you remember," Martha said slowly, "how there was a time when men used to speak about the earth our mother? It was Mother Earth, and they believed it. She was the source of life and being."

"She still is."

"You've sucked her dry," Martha said curiously. "When a woman is sucked dry, her children perish."

It was an odd and poetical thing to say, and, as I thought, in bad taste. I punished Martha by leaving Mrs. Gaffey with her, with the excuse that Max and I had some business matters to discuss, which indeed we did. We went into the new study in the new house and we lit fifty-cent cigars, and Max told me about the thing they had aptly named "Project Hades."

"The point is," Max said, "that I can get you into this at the very beginning. At the bottom. There are eleven companies involved–very solid and reputable companies"–he named them, and I was duly impressed–"who are putting up the capital for what will be a subsidiary of Thunder Inc. For their money they get a twenty-five-percent interest. There is also ten percent, in the form of stock warrants, put aside for consultation and advice, and you will understand why. I can fit you in for one and a half percent–roughly three quarters of a million–simply for a few weeks of your time, and we will pay all expenses, plus an opinion."

"It sounds interesting."

"It should sound more than that. If Project Hades works, your interest will increase tenfold within a matter of five years. It's the shortest cut to being a millionaire that I know."

"All right–I'm more than interested. Go on."

Gaffey took a map of Arizona out of his pocket, unfolded it, and pointed to a marked-off area. "Here," he said, "is what should–accordng to all our geological knowledge–be one of the richest oil-bearing areas in the country. Do you agree?"

"Yes, I know the area," I replied. "I've been over it. Its oil potential is purely theoretical. No one has ever brought in anything there—not even salt water. It's dry and dead."

"Why?"

I shrugged. "That's the way it is. If we could locate oil through geological premise and theory, you and I would both be richer than Getty. The fact of the matter is, as you well know, that sometimes it's there and sometimes it isn't. More often it isn't."

"Why? We know our job. We drill in the right places."

"What are you getting at, Max?"

"A speculation—particularly for this area. We have discussed this speculation for months. We have tested it as best we can. We have examined it from every possible angle. And now we are ready to blow about five million dollars to test our hypothesis—providing—"

"Providing what?"

"That your expert opinion agrees with ours. In other words, we've cast the die with you. You look at the situation and tell us to go ahead—we go ahead. You look at it and tell us it's a crock of beans—well, we fold our tents like the Arabs and silently steal away."

"Just on my say-so?"

"Just on your brains and know-how."

"Max, aren't you barking up the wrong tree? I'm a simple professor of geology at an unimportant western state university, and there are at least twenty men in the field who can teach me the right time—"

"Not in our opinion. Not on where the stuff is. We know who's in the field and we know their track records. You keep your light under a bushel, but we know what we want. So don't argue. It's either a deal or it isn't. Well?"

"How the devil can I answer you when I don't even know what you're talking about?"

"All right–I'll spell it out, quick and simple. The oil was there once, right where it should be. Then a natural convulsion–a very deep fault. The earth cracked and the oil flowed down, deep down, and now giant pockets of it are buried there where no drill can reach them."

"How deep?"

"Who knows? Fifteen, twenty miles."

"That's deep."

"Maybe deeper. When you think of that kind of distance under the surface, you're in a darker mystery than Mars or Venus–all of which you know."

"All of which I know." I had a bad, uneasy feeling, and some of it must have shown in my face.

"What's wrong?"

"I don't know. Why don't you leave it alone, Max?"

"Why?"

"Come on, Max–we're not talking about drilling for oil. Fifteen, twenty miles. There's a rig down near the Pecos in Texas and they've just passed the twenty-five-thousand-foot level, and that's about it. Oh, maybe another thousand, but you're talking about oil that's buried in one hundred thousand feet of crust. You can't drill for it; you can only go in and–"

"And what?"

"Blast it out."

"Of course–and how do you fault us for that? What's wrong with it? We know–or least we have good reason to believe–that there's a fissure that opened and closed. The oil should be under tremendous pressure. We put in an atom bomb–a bigger bomb than we ever used before—and we blast that fissure open again. Great God almighty, that should be the biggest gusher in all the history of gushers."

"You've drilled the hole already, haven't you, Max?"

"That's right."

"How deep?"

"Twenty-two thousand feet."

"And you have the bomb?"

Max nodded. "We have the bomb. We've been working on this for five years, and seven months ago the boys in Washington cleared the bomb. It's out there in Arizona waiting—"

"For what?"

"For you to look everything over and tell us to go ahead."

"Why? We have enough oil—"

"Like hell we have! You know damn well why—and do you imagine we can drop it now after all the money and time that's been invested in this?"

"You said you'd drop it if I said so."

"As a geologist in our pay, and I know you well enough to know what that means in terms of your professional skill and pride."

I stayed up half that night talking with Martha about it and trying to fit it into some kind of moral position. But the only thing I could come up with was the fact that here was one less atom bomb to murder man and destroy the life of the earth, and that I could not argue with. A day later I was at the drilling site in Arizona.

The spot was well chosen. From every point of view this was an oil explorer's dream, and I suppose that fact had been duly noted for the past half century, for there were the moldering remains of a hundred futile rigs, rotting patterns of wooden and metal sticks as far as one could see, abandoned shacks, trailers left with lost hopes, ancient trucks, rusting gears, piles of abandoned pipe—all testifying to the hope that springs eternal in the wildcatter's breast.

Thunder Inc. was something else, a great installation in the middle of the deep valley, a drilling rig larger and more complex than any I had ever seen, a wall to contain the oil should they fail to cap it immediately, a machine shop, a small generating plant, at least a hundred vehicles of various sorts, and perhaps fifty mobile homes. The very extent and vastness of the action here deep in the badlands was breathtaking; and I let Max know what I thought of his statement that all this would be abandoned if I said that the idea was worthless.

"Maybe yes—maybe no. What *do* you say?"

"Give me time."

"Absolutely, all the time you want."

Never have I been treated with such respect. I prowled all over the place and I rode a jeep around and about and back and forth and up into the hills and down again; but no matter how long I prowled and sniffed and estimated, mine would be no more than an educated guess. I was also certain that they would not give up the project if I disapproved and said that it would be a washout. They believed in me as a sort of oil-dowser, especially if I told them to go ahead. What they were really seeking was an expert's affirmation of their own faith. And that was apparent from the fact that they had already drilled an expensive twenty-two-thousand-foot hole and had set up all this equipment. If I told them they were wrong, their faith might be shaken a little, but they would recover and find themselves another dowser.

I told this to Martha when I telephoned her.

"Well, what do you honestly think?"

"It's oil country. But I'm not the first one to come up with that brilliant observation. The point is—does their explanation account for the lack of oil?"

"Does it?"

"I don't know. No one knows. And they're dangling a million dollars right in front of my nose."

"I can't help you," Martha said. "You've got to play this one yourself."

Of course she couldn't help me. No one could have helped me. It was too far down, too deeply hidden. We knew what the other side of the moon looked like and we knew something about Mars and other planets, but what have we ever known about ourselves and the place where we live?

The day after I spoke to Martha, I met with Max and his board of directors.

"I agree," I told them. "The oil should be there. My opinion is that you should go ahead and try the blast."

They questioned me after that for about an hour, but when you play the roll of a dowser, questions and answers become a sort of magical ritual. The plain fact of the matter is that no one had ever exploded a bomb of such power at such a depth, and until it was done, no one knew what would happen.

I watched the preparations for the explosion with great interest. The bomb, with its implosion casing, was specially made for this task—or remade would be a better way of putting it—very long, almost twenty feet, very slim. It was armed after it was in the rigging, and then the board of directors, engineers, technicians, newspapermen, Max, and myself retreated to the concrete shelter and control stations, which had been built almost a mile away from the shaft. Closed-circuit television linked us with the hole; and while no one expected the explosion to do any more than jar the earth heavily at the surface, the Atomic Energy Commission specified the precautions we took.

We remained in the shelter for five hours while the bomb made its long descent—until at last our instruments told us that it rested on the bottom of the drill hole. Then we had a simple countdown, and the chairman of the board pressed the red button. Red and white buttons are man's glory. Press a white button and a bell rings or an electric light goes on; press a red button and the hellish force of a sun comes into being—this time five miles beneath the earth's surface.

Perhaps it was this part and point in the earth's surface; perhaps there was no other place where exactly the same thing would have happened; perhaps the fault that drained away the oil was a deeper fault than we had ever imagined. Actually we will never know; we only saw what we saw, watching it through the closed-circuit TV. We saw the earth swell. The swell rose up like a bubble—a bubble about two hundred yards in diameter—and then the surface of the bubble dissipated in a column of dust or smoke that rose up perhaps five hundred feet from the valley bottom, stayed a moment with the lowering sun behind it, like the very column of fire out of Sinai, and then lifted whole and broke suddenly in the wind. Even in the shelter we heard the screaming rumble of sound, and as the face of the enormous hole that the dust had left cleared, there bubbled up a column of oil perhaps a hundred feet in diameter. Or was it oil?

The moment we saw it, a tremendous cheer went up in the shelter, and then the cheer cut off in its own echo. Our closed-circuit system was color television, and this column of oil was bright red.

"Red oil," someone whispered.

Then it was quiet.

"When can we get out?" someone else demanded.

"Another ten minutes."

The dust was up and away in the opposite direction, and for ten minutes we stood and watched the bright red oil bubble out of the hole, forming a great pond within the retaining walls, and filling the space with amazing rapidity and lapping over the walls, for the flow must have been a hundred thousand gallons a second or even more, and then outside of the walls and a thickness of it all across the valley floor, rising so quickly that from above, where we were, we saw that we would be cut off from the entire installation. At that point we didn't wait, but took our chances with the radiation and raced down the desert hillside toward the hole and the mobile homes and the trucks—but not quickly enough. We came to a stop at the edge of a great lake of red oil.

"It's not red oil," someone said.

"Goddamnit, it's not oil!"

"The hell it's not! It's oil!"

We were moving back as it spread and rose and covered the trucks and houses, and then it reached a gap in the valley and poured through and down across the desert, into the darkness of the shadows that the big rocks threw—flashing red in the sunset and later black in the darkness.

Someone touched it and put a hand to his mouth.

"It's blood."

Max was next to me. "He's crazy," Max said.

Someone else said that it was blood.

I put a finger into the red fluid and raised it to my nose. It was warm, almost hot, and there was no mistaking the smell of hot, fresh blood. I tasted it with the tip of my tongue.

"What is it?" Max whispered.

The others gathered around now—silent, with the red sun setting across the red lake and the red reflected on our faces, our eyes glinting with the red.

"Jesus God, what is it?" Max demanded.

"It's blood," I replied.

"From where?"

Then we were all silent.

We spent the night on the top of the butte where the shelter had been built, and in the morning, all around us, as far as we could see, there was a hot, steaming sea of red blood, the smell so thick and heavy that we were all sick from it; and all of us vomited half a dozen times before the helicopters came for us and took us away.

The day after I returned home, Martha and I were sitting in the living room, she with a book and I with the paper, where I had read about their trying to cap the thing, except that even with diving suits they could not get down to where it was; and she looked up from her book and said:

"Do you remember the thing about the mother?"

"What thing?"

"A very old thing. I think I heard once that it was half as old as time, or maybe a Greek fable or something of the sort—but anyway, the mother has one son, who is the joy of her heart and all the rest that a son could be to a mother, and then the son falls in love with or under the spell of a beautiful and wicked woman—very wicked and very beautiful. And he desires to please her, oh, he does indeed, and he says to her, 'Whatever you desire, I will bring it to you'—"

"Which is nothing to say to any woman, but ever," I put in.

"I won't quarrel with that," Martha said mildly, "because when he does put it to her, she replies that what she desires most on this earth is the living heart of his mother, plucked from her breast. So what does this worthless and murderous idiot male do, but race home to his mother, and then out with a knife, ripping her breast to belly and tearing the living heart out of her body—"

"I don't like your story."

"—and with the heart in his hand, he blithely dashes back toward his ladylove. But on the way through the forest he catches his toe on a root, stumbles, and falls headlong, the mother's heart knocked out of his hand. And as he pulls himself up and approaches the heart, it says to him, 'Did you hurt yourself when you fell, my son?'"

"Lovely story. What does it prove?"

"Nothing, I suppose. Will they ever stop the bleeding? Will they ever close the wound?"

"I don't think so."

"Then will your mother bleed to death?"

"My mother?"

"Yes."

"Oh."

"My mother," Martha said. "Will she bleed to death?"

"I suppose so."

"That's all you can say—I suppose so?"

"What else?"

"Suppose you had told them not to go ahead?"

"You asked me that twenty times, Martha. I told you. They would have gotten another dowser."

"And another? And another?"

"Yes."

"Why?" she cried out. "For God's sake, why?"

"I don't know."

"But you lousy men know everything else."

"Mostly we only know how to kill it. That's not everything else. We never learned to make anything alive."

"And now it's too late," Martha said.

"It's too late, yes," I agreed, and I went back to reading the paper. But Martha just sat there, the open book in her lap, looking at me; and then after a while she closed the book and went upstairs to bed.

tomorrow's wall street journal

At precisely eight forty-five in the morning, carrying a copy of tomorrow's *Wall Street Journal* under his arm, the devil knocked at the door of Martin Chesell's apartment. The devil was a handsome middle-aged businessman, dressed in a two hundred-dollar gray sharksin suit, forty-five-dollar shoes, a custom-made shirt, and a twenty-five-dollar iron-gray Italian silk tie. He wore a forty-dollar hat, which he took off politely as the door opened.

Martin Chesell, who lived on the eleventh floor of one of those high-rise apartments that grow like mushrooms on Second Avenue in the seventies and eighties, was wearing pants and a shirt, neither with a lineage of place or price. His wife, Doris, had just said to him, "What kind of a nut is it at this hour? You better look through the peephole."

"Drop dead," he replied as he looked through the peephole.

Knowing a good tie and shirt when he saw them, Martin Chesell opened the door and asked the devil what he wanted.

"I'm the devil," the devil answered politely. "And I am here to make a deal for tomorrow's *Wall Street Journal*."

"Buzz off, buster," Martin said in disgust. "The hospital's

over by the river, six blocks from here. Go sign yourself in."

"I am the devil," the devil insisted. "I am really the devil, scout's honor." Then he pushed Martin aside and entered the apartment, being rather stronger than people.

"Martin, who is it?" his wife yelled–and then she came to see. She was dressed to go to her job at Bonwit's, where she sold dresses until her feet died–every day about four-twenty–and she saw enough faces in a day's time to smell the devil when he was near her.

"Ask your wife," the devil said pleasantly.

"It wouldn't surprise me," said Doris. "What are you peddling, mister?"

"Tomorrow's *Wall Street Journal*," the devil repeated amiably. "Everyman's desire and dream."

"It's an old tired saw," Martin Chesell said. "It's been used to death. Not only have a dozen bad stories been written to the same point, but the *New Yorker* ran a cartoon on the same subject. A tired old bum looks down, and there's tomorrow's *Wall Street Journal* at his feet."

"That's where I picked up the notion." The devil nodded eagerly. "Basically, I am conservative, but one can't go on forever with the same old thing, you know." He walked sprightly into their living room, merely glancing into the bedroom with its unmade bed, and measuring with another glance the cheap, tasteless furniture, and then spread the paper on the table. Martin and Doris followed him and looked at the date.

"They print those headlines in a place on Forty-eighth Street," Doris said knowingly.

"Ah! And the inside pages as well?" The devil riffled the pages.

"Suppose you let me have a look at the last page?" Martin said.

"Ah—that costs."

"Mister, go away. There is no devil and you're some kind of a nut. My wife has to go to work."

"But you don't? No job. Bless your hearts, what does a devil do to prove himself. My driving license? Or this?" Blue points of fire danced on his fingernails. "Or this?" Two horns appeared on his forehead, glistened a moment, and then disappeared. "Or this?" He held up finger and thumb and a twenty-dollar antique gold piece appeared between them. He tossed it to Martin, who caught it and examined it carefully.

"Tricks, tricks," said the devil. "Look into your own heart if you doubt me, my boy. Do we deal? I sell—you buy—one copy of tomorrow's *Wall Street Journal.* Yes?"

"What price?" Doris demanded, precise, businesslike, and to the point, while her husband still stared bemused at the coin.

"The usual price. The price never changes. A human soul."

"Why?" Martin snapped, holding out the coin.

"Keep it, my son," the devil said.

"Why a human soul? What do you do with them? Collect them? Frame them."

"They have their uses, oh yes, indeed. It would make for a long, complicated explanation, but we value them."

"I don't believe I have a soul," Martin said bluntly.

"Then what loss if you sell it to me? To sell what you do not own without deceiving the purchaser, that is good business, Martin—all profit and no loss."

"I'll sell mine," Doris said.

"Oh? Would you? But that won't do."

"Why not?"

"No—it just wouldn't do." He looked at his watch, a beautiful old pocket watch, gold and set with rubies and with little imps crawling all over it. "You know, I don't have all the time in the world. You must decide."

"For Christ's sake," Doris said, "sell him your damn soul or do we spend the rest of our lives in this lousy three-room rathole? Because if that's the case, you spend them alone, Marty boy. I am sick to death of your sitting around on your ass while I work my own butt off. You're a loser, sweety, and this is probably the last chance."

"Good girl," the devil said approvingly. "She has a head on her shoulders, Martin."

"How do I know—"

"Martin, Martin, what do you have to lose?"

"My soul."

"Whose existence you sensibly doubt. Come, Martin—"

"How?"

"Old-fashioned but simple. I have the contract here, all very direct and legal. You read it. A pinprick, a drop of blood on your signature, and tomorrow's *Wall Street Journal* is yours."

Martin Chesell read the contract. A pin appeared like magic in the devil's hand. A thumb was pricked, and Martin found himself smearing a drop of blood across his signature.

"All of which makes it legal and binding," the devil said, smiling and handing Martin the paper. Doris forgot her job and Martin forgot his erstwhile soul, and they flung the paper open with trembling hands, riffled to the last page but one, where the New York Stock Exchange companies and prices were printed, and scanned the list. The devil watched this with benign amusement, until suddenly Martin whirled and cried:

"You bastard—this is a rotten day. Everything is down."

"Hardly, Martin, hardly," the devil replied, soothingly. "Everything is never down. Some are up, some are down. I will admit that today is hardly the most inspiring of days, but there is a surprise or two. Just look at old Mother Bell."

"Who?"

"American Telephone," the devil said. "Look at it, Martin."

Martin looked. "Up four points," he whispered. "That makes no sense at all. American Telephone hasn't jumped four points in a day since Alexander Graham Bell invented it."

"Oh, it has, Martin. Yes, indeed. You see, until two o'clock today, it will just dilly-dally along the way it does every other day, and then at two precisely the management will announce a two-for-one split. Yes, indeed, Martin—two for one. Just read those prices again, and you will see that it touches a high of five dollars and seventy-five cents over the two o'clock price, even though it closes at a profit of only four points. So you see, Martin, if you sell at the high, you can clear five dollars and better, which is a very nice return for an in-and-out deal. No reason at all why you shouldn't be a very rich man before today is over, Martin. No reason at all."

"Marty," Doris shouted, "we're going to do it. We're going to make it, Marty. This is the big one, the big red apple—the one we've been waiting for. Oh, Marty, I love you, I love you, I love you."

The devil smiled with pleasure, put on his forty-dollar hat, and departed. They hardly noticed that he had gone, so eager were they to be properly dressed to make a million. Doris tied Martin's tie—something she had not done for a long time. Martin admired the dress she changed into and quietly agreed when she snapped at him:

"You keep that newspaper in an inside pocket, Marty. Nobody sees it—and I mean nobody."

"Right you are, baby."

"Marty, what do we go for? Five dollars a share—is that it?"

"That's it, baby. Suppose we pick up twenty thousand shares—that's one hundred thousand dollars, baby. One hundred thousand bright, green dollars."

"Marty, have you lost your mind? This is it—the one and only—and you talk about one hundred thousand dollars. We pick up a hundred thousand shares, and then we got half a million. Half a million dollars, Marty. Beautiful, lean dollars."

"All right, baby. But I'm not sure you can buy a hundred thousand shares of a stock like American Tel and Tel without influencing the price. If we drive the price up—"

"We can't drive the price up, Marty."

"How do you know? What makes you such a goddamn stock market genius?"

"Marty, maybe I don't know one thing about the market—but I know how it closes today. Honey, don't you see—we have tomorrow's *Wall Street Journal*. We know. No matter how many shares of that stock you buy, it is going to stay put until two o'clock and then it's going to go up five dollars and seventy-five cents. Isn't that what he said?"

Marty opened the paper and concentrated on it. "Right!" he cried triumphantly. "Says so right here—no movement until two o'clock—and then zoom."

"So we could buy two hundred thousand shares and make a cool million."

"Right, baby—oh, you are so right!"

"Two hundred thousand shares then—right, Marty?"

"I hear you, kid."

They took a cab downtown to the brokerage office of Smith, Haley and Penderson on Fifty-third Street. When you have it, you spend it. "Lunch today at the Four Seasons?" Doris asked him. "Right, baby. Right, baby." Rich people are happy people. When he and Doris marched up to the desk of Frank Gibson, their poise and pleasure were contagious. Frank Gibson had gone to college with Martin and had supervised his few unhappy stock market transactions, and while he did not consider Martin one of his more valuable contacts, he found himself smiling back and telling them that it was good to see them.

"Both of you," he said. "Day off, Doris?"

Doris indicated that days off were the farthest things from her mind, and Martin outlined his purpose with that superior and secure sense that the buyer in quantity always has. But instead of leaping with joy, Gibson stared at him unhappily.

"Please sit down," Gibson said.

They sat down.

"If I understand you, Marty, you want to buy two hundred thousand shares of American Telephone. You're putting me on."

"No. We're dead serious."

"Even if you're serious, you're putting me on, Marty," Gibson said. "This kind of goofing—well, someone gets upset. Someone gets angry."

"Look, Frank," Martin said, "you are a broker. You are a customer's man. I am a customer. I come to buy, and you tell me politely to go take a walk."

"Marty," Gibson said patiently, "that much American Telephone adds up to over ten million dollars. That means you have to have at least six million, give or take a few, to back it up. So what's the use, Marty? Take the gag somewhere else."

"Then you won't take my order?"

"Marty–Marty, no one will take your order. Because you got to be some kind of nut to even talk that way when I know that you and Doris between you–you got maybe twenty cents."

"That's a hell of a thing to say!"

"Is it true?"

"For heaven's sake, Marty," Doris put in, "come clean with him and get the thing on the road. Here it is, Frank. We got inside dope that Telephone is going up five points this afternoon. At two o'clock today they are going to announce a stock split–and it will go."

"How do you know?"

"We know."

"Nobody knows. That rumor has been around for months. Telephone is the blandest, dullest piece of action on the market. You are asking for a day sale, and this firm would not stand for even a little one. It's out of the question."

"You mean you won't sell me stock?"

"A hundred shares of Telephone–sure. You have an account with us. Buy a hundred shares. Don't be greedy–"

They stalked out while Gibson was talking. The next stop was Doris' brother, who was a lawyer and made a good living out of it and could have gone on living if he never saw Martin Chesell again.

"I should underwrite six million of credit for you? You got to be kidding."

"I'm not kidding, I'm dead serious," Martin replied, telling himself, "You, you son of a bitch, what a pleasure it would be to toss you out on your fat ass if you came pleading to me. Time—just give me time."

"Am I permitted to ask what for?" his brother-in-law said.

"To make an investment in the market," Martin said. "I am desperate. It is eleven o'clock. This is the first real chance I ever had. Please," he pleaded, "do you want me to get down on my knees?"

"It would be an interesting position for a snotty guy like you," the brother-in-law said. "I should be happy to underwrite seventy-five cents for you, Martin. For a whole buck, I write it off immediately."

"You may be my brother," Doris said, "but to me you are a louse. May I spell it—l-o-u-s-e."

It was eleven-thirty when they got to the branch of the Chase Manhattan on upper Madison. Martin had been in college with the son of the present manager, and once he had introduced himself and Doris, the manager listened politely.

"Of course, we would be happy to lend you the money," he agreed. "In any amount you wish—providing you offer acceptable collateral."

"Would American Telephone stock be acceptable collateral?" Doris asked eagerly.

"The very best. And I think we might even lend you up to eighty percent of the market value."

"See, Marty!" Doris exclaimed. "I knew we'd do it! Now can we get the money immediately?"

"I think so—at least within fifteen minutes. Do you have the stock with you?"

Doris' face fell, while Martin explained that they were going to use the money to buy the stock.

"Well, that's a little different, isn't it? I am afraid it makes the loan impossible—unless you have sufficient stock already in your possession. It doesn't have to be American Telephone. Any listed security—"

"You don't understand," Martin pleaded, watching the clock on the wall. "We got to buy that stock before two o'clock."

"I am sure you have good reason to. But we can't help you."

"Lousy crumb," Martin said when they got outside. "He stinks! The whole lousy Chase Manhattan stinks! You got a friend at Chase Manhattan, you don't need enemies. You know what I'd like to do, go in there up to the window and—stick 'em up!—that's what I'd like to do."

Neither First National City nor Chemical New York proved any more flexible on the question of collateral, nor was Merrill Lynch disposed to open an account and plunge into a massive day sale. One forty-five P.M. found them back at the offices of Smith, Haley and Penderson, pleading anew with Frank Gibson.

"I got a job," Gibson told them. "You may not believe me, but being a customer's man just happens to be a job. I don't interfere with you, so just let me do my job."

"It's a quarter to two," Martin begged him.

"Oh, Jesus—show him the damn *Wall Street Journal*," Doris snapped.

"Why don't you drop dead?"

"Why don't you get one little brain in your head? It's ten minutes to two. Show him the paper."

Martin took out the paper and shoved it at Gibson. "There—tomorrow's *Wall Street Journal.* All markets—complete closing prices."

"You're both out of your minds. What do I have to do? Make a scene? Call the cops?"

"Just look at the date? Am I asking so much? Jesus God, if I was drowning would you stretch out a hand for me? I'm asking you to look at the date."

"O.K.—so I look at the date." Gibson picked up the paper and looked at the date. Then he stared at the date. Then he turned the paper around and looked at the date on the back page. Then he opened it.

"Marty, where did you get this?"

"Now you believe me. Now Marty's not a lousy creep any more. Now Marty's your buddy boy. Now will you buy the goddamn stock?"

"Marty, I can't. Even if I thought this paper wasn't phony—"

"Phony! Do you know—"

His voice died away. Gibson was staring at the screened flash news at the front of the office, where suddenly the news had appeared that the directors of American Telephone had decided upon a two-for-one stock split, pending approval of stockholders.

"Will you buy the stock?" Martin whimpered. "Oh, dear Jesus, will you please buy the stock?"

"Marty—I can't."

"It's up two points already," Doris said. "Why don't I kill myself? Oh, no—I couldn't jump in front of a subway train or anything like that. No, sir—not me. I had to marry Chesell."

At two, when the market closed, American Telephone was

four points over its opening price. At four-fifteen, the Chesells had one of their minor fights. If they had not been so done in with the day, it might have been a major fight. As it was, there was nothing physical, only a few recriminations, one word leading to another. Doris began the peroration by concluding:

"Drop dead–that's all."

"So long as you understand the feeling is mutual."

"Lovely–and I have had it, ducky. Words cannot portray my feelings for you. You disgust me. You also turn my stomach. You also stink–and now I intend to have a nap. So just get out of here!"

Martin went into the living room, and she slammed the door behind him–and there was a gentle knock at the door to the apartment. Martin opened the door, and there was the devil.

"Greetings, my lad," he said with great good nature.

"You got one hell of a nerve!" Martin exclaimed. "You miserable son of a bitch–after what you did to me, to come back here!"

"What I did? Martin, Martin, you are understandably angry–but that kind of wild talk–not good."

"You tricked me into that."

"Martin, my boy," the devil said kindly, "did we or did we not make an honest trade, a bargain in kind, merchandise given, merchandise taken? Did we not?"

"You knew what would happen."

"And just what did happen, Martin? Why get so upset? I gave you the *Wall Street Journal* for tomorrow and you found yourself not unexpectedly short of cash. Lesson number one–money makes money. How easily learned–and you complain."

"Because I blew my one lousy chance," Martin said. "One lousy chance out of a whole lifetime, and I blew it. One chance to come out on top, and I threw it away."

"Martin."

"No, it doesn't matter to you. Well–me, I am sick and tired of you, so out. Just get the hell out!"

"Martin," the devil said placatingly.

"Out!"

"Really, Martin."

"Are you trying to tell me you didn't know what would happen?"

"Martin, of course I knew what would happen. I have been at this so long, and people are so wretchedly predictable. But what happened today is of no importance."

"No importance?"

"None whatsoever. The really important thing is that you sold me your soul, Martin. That's the nitty-gritty of it. Riches? No problem. Wealth, power, success? No problem, Martin. It all follows. Once you have sold your soul to me, everything comes to you–everything, Martin. Dear lad–you look so blue, so morbid. Cheer up. The *Wall Street Journal*–who needs it? Do you want a tip for tomorrow? Cimeron Lead–four dollars a share. It will close at seven. Buy a few shares; pin money, but buy a few shares."

"With what?" Martin asked sourly.

"Money–dear Martin, there is money wherever you look. For example, you have a bit of insurance on your wife, don't you?"

"We each have a policy for twenty thousand."

"Very nice beginning money, Martin. Fortunes have been

built on less. And you don't really like her at all, do you?"

"Why wouldn't you make a deal for her soul this morning?" Martin asked suddenly.

"Dear Martin—her soul is worthless. In the five years of your marriage you have shriveled it to nothing. You have a talent for destruction, Martin. Her soul is almost nonexistent, and she's not very pleasant to be with, is she, Martin?"

Martin nodded.

"And she's so despondent today—it would be understandable that she should leap from an eleventh-story window. Poor girl, but some win and some lose, Martin."

"I wouldn't collect on the insurance for ten days," Martin said.

"Good thinking. I like that. Now you are using your head, lad. Rest assured, I have a better tip for next week. Tips, opportunities, good liquor, rich good, uncomplaining women, and money—so much money. Dear Martin, why do you hesitate?"

Martin went into the bedroom, closing the door behind him. There were the sounds of a short scuffle—and then a long, awful scream. When Martin came out of the bedroom, the devil sighed and said, "Poor boy, you'll be despondent tonight. We must dine together. You will be my guest—of course. And to console you—"

He took out of his inside breast pocket a neatly folded copy of the *Wall Street Journal.*

"For a week from Wednesday—ten days," he said.

the interval

Few will face it, but there is a beginning and an end; that's the way it is, and after you turn fifty, it stares you in the face. You read the obituary pages and you find that people of your own age and people even younger than you are dying, and then it closes in on you and you can be alone, the way I was. When you are decently married for a long, long while you are fortunate to go first; but if you are left behind, you keep looking at yourself and wondering what you are waiting for.

I went up to northern Connecticut, to the foothills of the Berkshires, to see about putting our summer place on the market; but even as I spoke to the local real estate man, I found that I had no feelings one way or another about the place. I was indifferent to price or terms, and since I was so obliging a client, the broker parted with a few pleasantries and then said obliquely, as many New Englanders would:

"How about them fellers up on the moon?"

These Yankees change the subject to suit them; I was talking about the house but he wanted to talk about the moon—meaning he had regard for me or that he was returning my favor of obliging him, in his peculiar Connecticut manner. He didn't care what I thought or felt about the moon; he himself felt queasy, and I wondered whether the whole world didn't feel a bit queasy.

When I didn't answer, he said, "Fine, full moon tonight."

I nodded and left him, and then drove along Main Street to Old Turkey Gobbler Road, and then three miles to the house. The house had stood on its knoll for two hundred years, and during that time a dozen owners had cherished it and changed this and added that; and we had cherished it, too, for the nineteen years we had it.

All the time I had looked at it in the past, it had always been a house warm inside, alive, full of the past and the lives and the spirit of all the kids who had played and grown up there and the smell of the good things that had been cooked there and the passion of the sex and the love and the hate that had happened there, the hungers satisfied and unsatisfied, the longings, the fulfillment, the disappointments, the fears, the apprehensions—so it had been all the times I had seen it in the past. But now it was quiet without passion. It was only a box, and inside it was very cold, for the edge of winter had touched it already, and New England winter comes quick and hard in the Berkshires.

But this winter had an edge of icy cold that was furtive rather than literal. You felt it creeping through your bones, and before any frostbite touched your skin, you felt it at the edge of your heart. I had begun to shiver and I wanted a fire desperately, and I went out to the woodbox which I had filled with good, dry kindling the summer before. I made my fire and burned a few papers to start a blast up the chimney, and then added the kindling and put on top of that three thick old pieces of gray birch, or the silver birch, as some call it—and then indeed heat came from the big stone box. But there was still a chill in the room.

It was late afternoon and the light was beginning to fade. I prowled through the old empty house, looking for this or that to take back to the city; but there was nothing I wanted particularly, not even the first manuscripts of my very early plays and books. The battered old typewriter was a good, rare Underwood out of the thirties, but I had another in New York. Some day, perhaps, I would ship away the pictures and books, but not now. Some day when I cared more.

The moon rose, so strong and silver-bright that the day seemed not to fade or perish but only to turn color, and the moonlight turned bright the faces of the mountains to the north of me. Here and there was a thin cover of snow on the hillsides, and where the snow was you could see the distant slopes in detail.

I lit my pipe and smoked and stared at the leaping flames of the fire, and I think that in some way I knew what was coming. Because for me it was no great surprise to glance out of the window and see what I saw. I had knocked out my pipe onto the hearth, and I got up and walked to the broad windows that faced north, and I saw that it was finished and that they were picking up the scenery, rolling it up, either for good and to be disposed of however they dispose of such things, or to be used again elsewhere.

I mentioned before that it was a startlingly clear night, as if they could make white, incandescent moonlight for their own needs, and I suppose I could see a long way north. In any case, I saw clearly how the forested slopes were being rolled up, the way one might roll up a thick and unusual carpet, leaving underneath the gray, sere stuff that the riders to the moon had seen and described with such loathing. The green countryside was being taken up in great pieces, miles wide, and wherever the rolling up and lifting away was finished, the dry, dead gray stuff remained.

I did not watch for long, because I felt almost immediately that I must not witness the finish of this alone. I had to be with others. I had to pass a word. I had to comment, to speculate, to bewail, perhaps, to doubt my own eyes, to plead for some explanation other than the simple and obvious fact that the play was over and the curtain had come down—and because of this I bolted out of the house and into my car.

The car started easily, and I sent it plunging over the dirt road toward Route 22, over the shortest way, which would connect through the Wankhaus Overpass, a dirt road over a shoulder that linked the Old Turkey Gobbler Road with South Pike Road and so to Route 22. But they took up the Wankhaus Overpass; they had humor, and they could be bothered with small games, but I don't suppose they were vengeful. They left me alone there, and I sat in my car, staring through the windshield at the gray pumice that remained after they had taken up the road and the trees and the rocks, rolling it back and away and then casting it off somewhere in the wings. I mean, they let me back up, which wasn't vengeful, while the wind blew gray powder over my car and filled my nostrils with the dry, dead smell of it. I had to back up for over two hundred yards before I was able to turn into South Pike, but with three miles more to drive than would have been the case the other way, and then they let me find my way to Route 22. They were busy to the north and the west, and there I saw a whole town, factories, motor lodges, main street, Civil War monument, new business machines plant, car dealers—everything rolled up and dragged away. But silently. Well, my windows were up and I was too far away to hear people screaming. If they screamed; I didn't know, you see, because I had not uttered a sound, never protested or wailed or prayed or pleaded.

It surprised me as I drove south along Route 22 and then onto the Saw Mill River Parkway that I saw no other cars. Was it later than I could have imagined? I felt for my watch, and then I found that I had left it behind at the house, so I really had no idea at all of what time it was.

I was impressed myself by how well I drove, how fast, and with such quiet control—all things considered—and without undue excitement and panic. The Saw Mill River Parkway is one of the older Westchester parkways, two rather narrow lanes in each direction and not built for speed, but rather meandering over the hills like an old carriage road; yet I was able to build my speed up to and past seventy miles an hour—and still in my rearview mirror I could see tracts of houses rolled up and flung aside, hillsides stripped, and even the road behind me rolled up as I left it. But not at seventy miles an hour, and by the time I reached the Hawthorne Circle I could no longer see where they were gathering up the scenery and putting it away.

Even at the circle there were no cars, and past the circle I cut into the Tappan Zee approach, and then, crossing it, down onto the Thruway. Never before had I seen the Tappan Zee approach without traffic, without the endless stream of heavy trucks thundering to and from it, yet tonight the road was empty—and I had a sudden stab of fear that they might have picked up the Thruway as they had picked up the connecting road back in the foothills. If I thought of them at all, I thought of them as stagehands with a gross, bulky physical sense of humor, stagehands who loved nothing better than the embarrassment of this or that actor; for whatever the stagehand is, he creates nothing and performs nothing, only watches with the knowledge that his only mark of superiority is that he will be there for the next show and the show after that.

But the Thruway was there, alone, empty, as if this night had seven strange hours when all the world slept; and my car alone raced down it, seventy, eighty miles an hour, the wide lanes empty and bright in the moonlight.

I braked to a screaming stop where the tollgate was, but to no purpose. The booths were empty, and there was no one to pay or to ask for the toll. Beyond that, where the big complex of the Cross County Shopping Center had been, was the dry, windblown pumice of the moon; a big strip had been sliced out, rolled up and taken away, a strip that curved around to include the racetrack. But when I reached the city, nothing had been disturbed or moved. Except that mostly the city was dark. Here and there, in this apartment house or that one, a lighted window shone; yet mostly the city was dark and the Major Deegan Expressway was empty—empty all the way to the Triborough Bridge, where there was light but no cars and no toll takers. I came to the East Side Drive and drove downtown, no longer racing, but slowly and all alone, and then I left the drive and crossed through the city streets where I saw a slow-moving prowl car but nothing else alive or moving. I felt an impulse to drive up alongside the prowl car and tell them or let them tell me; but I knew it was wrong to do that.

I went where I knew I would go—to the Mummers', where I had been a member for thirty-three years. I drove down Lexington Avenue to Gramercy Park, and there was a parking space directly in front of the club. I had been so anxious that it might be dark, as almost every other building was, but no, not at all; it was well-lit, and the door was opened by old Simon, the doorman, who welcomed me gravely and took my hat and coat as if this night were no different from any other night and said very quietly:

"There are quite a few members here, sir—mostly down in the bar. We are still serving in the dining room, nothing very spectacular but sandwiches and hot soup."

"That's odd," I remarked. "Dining room at this hour."

"Well, it's an odd night, sir. You will admit that."

"Quite odd. Yes, indeed."

I went downstairs to the bar, which was quite crowded, and at the pool table half a dozen members sipped beer and seriously watched a serious game of pool. I don't know why, but it was always the thing to have beer if you watched at the pool table, only I had never remarked on it before. I did now, thinking what an excellent setting for a first act this would make. I don't remember that anyone had ever staged the first act of a play as the basement at the Mummers', yet there was no one in the theater—no male person, that is—who had not spent at least an evening here. The game was between Jerry Goldman and Steve Cunningham, both of them hustlers of a sort and good enough to make a living off it if they had to. I watched them for a moment or two, nodding to old acquaintances, and then I edged into the bar between Jack Finney and Bert Avery, the stage designer, and asked Robert, the bartender, for a double rye whiskey over ice.

"Old Overhalt?" Robert asked.

"That will do nicely."

Finney was quietly drunk. He greeted me gently and politely; he was a great Irish gentleman with the blood of knights in his veins, like all Irishmen whom one loves, and a splendid character actor. Bert Avery asked me if I had just driven down from Connecticut.

"Yes. Thank heavens I am here. It was cold and lonely up there."

"Were they taking it up?"

"Yes—from the hillsides, you know, and then behind me on the Saw Mill River Parkway. They had taken out most of New Rochelle, from the shopping center right back in."

"Irv Goldstein flew up from Miami," Finney said sadly. "His was the last flight. They had taken up most of Florida. I've had good times in Miami; some don't like it, but I always have, for it is a fine place of loose-living, easygoing people. But it is flat, you know, oh, devilishly flat, and Goldstein says that they were rolling it up from the north, just nasty and uncaring, the whole length of the state rolled up like an old piece of carpet."

"Goldstein said it looked like the moon underneath," Bert Avery added, "with craters and things like that that had been covered over, I guess the way you have a lousy floor on a stage so you carpet it, and what the hell, it's a few hundred dollars more, and that's not going to make the difference between closing first night or running for a decent while."

"You are a fine manager," said Finney. "You are a gentleman at it. It is an honor to work for you."

Robert came over with another whiskey sour for Bert Avery, listened to the last of our conversation, and then asked whether we did not think that they might be putting it away and saving it for another performance.

"Somewhere else?" I thought about it for a moment. "Then they would be changing the cast, wouldn't they?"

"That's very sad, sir."

"The kids come to the theater with joy," Finney observed, "but in all truth it's a sad profession. One day you look up at the scenery, and it looks just as shoddy as all hell, and damnit, you say to yourself, has it always been this way, or is it turning lousy or is it inside of my own aching head?"

"All of them," Avery agreed.

I finished my drink and went over to the pool table, where Steve Cunningham was making one of those damned impossible cushion shots and no one was even breathing.

Of course, people never behave the way you expect them to, and these were all people who knew about it, and as a matter of fact, there was Goldstein standing very close to Cunningham, his eyes fixed upon the ball as if nothing in the whole world was as important as gauging the angle of ball to cushion and ball to side pocket; and yet they all had relatives, children, wives, brothers, sisters, mothers, fathers; but against all of that, the same thing had apparently brought them here as had brought me.

Cunningham made his shot, perfectly, ball to cushion to pocket, and there was a whisper of approval but no applause. I nudged Goldstein.

"Hungry?"

He nodded.

"They have soup and sandwiches upstairs, I hear."

"All right."

We climbed the stairs to the dining room, picking a quiet corner table. The room wasn't empty, but then neither was it crowded—oh, maybe a dozen members eating or simply relaxed and talking. One of them had lit a cigar, and I saw Goldstein frowning in disapproval. I agreed with him. There was an unwritten rule that while a cigarette or a pipe was proper at the table, cigars were to be taken to the lounge where one could have coffee or brandy or whatever one wished. I saw no reason to break the custom tonight, and I guess we were both rather pleased when one of the waiters came over and whispered something to the member, who then nodded and put the cigar out. Our own waiter said to us:

"I'm afraid there's very little choice at this point. The soup is canned. We have ham sandwiches or ham and Swiss, but only white bread, which you can have toasted. We also have some Canadian cheddar and Bath Biscuits. And the coffee is very good, sir. We keep making it freshly."

"I'll have the cheese and biscuits," I said.

"And you, Mr. Goldstein?"

"The same—yes. Would you have any Italian coffee?"

"I'm afraid not, Mr. Goldstein. You know, we make it only for dinner."

He left for the food, and Goldstein said, smiling slightly, "You know, we're good actors. All of us. Naturally, there's a difference between the dilettante and the professional, but we're all quite good, don't you think?"

"I never thought of it quite that way."

"No, of course not. But this thing of Italian coffee only for dinner—well, now!"

"Yes, oh, yes," I agreed. "I hear you flew up from Miami."

"Yes. Very good flight. Very smooth. I dislike flying, but this was very smooth."

"Vacation?"

"No, no indeed. You know, I thought I would do one of those Jewish comic-tragic things about a Miami Beach hotel. You know the kind of thing, mostly schmaltz and bad jokes and maybe two percent validity so your audience will shed a tear or two if they're in the right mood. It's very much my line, and having done one on a Second Avenue restaurant and two on the Garment District, I find it the path of least resistance. Oh, it's not playwriting in your terms, but it does want a bit of skill and a bit of staging, and there's never been a good one about Miami. I found some delicious stuff—" His voice trailed away.

"And on the way back they were rolling up Florida?"

"Yes."

"It must have been an odd thing to see. From the air, I mean."

"Damned odd. Oh, yes. I mean, it was like an old piece of carpet. You know, at twenty-five thousand feet your whole scale changes."

"I wonder what they'll do with New York?"

"I suppose it's been done already in some places—I mean Rome or London or even Boston. You drove in from New England, I hear. Boston?"

I shook my head. "We could call someone—"

"No one does. You know how you can never get at a phone on a busy day. All four of them are yours to choose from."

"I just don't like to think that they'll roll it up."

"No. I can see that."

"They might move it aside somewhere."

"I'd like to think so. You were born in Maine, weren't you?"

I nodded.

"Well, I'm the third generation born right here in the city. I hate to think that it will be all smashed up."

"We're simply being sentimental. That's no use, is it?"

"No use at all."

The waiter brought our food. The cheese was good and I've always liked Bath Biscuits, and I was hungry; but Goldstein barely touched his food. He sat in silence for a while, and then he said:

"I get a bit indignant over it, and then I remember our profession. We have no right to be indignant over it, have we?"

"You know, I read a good bit of history," I replied, "and the people of the theater always occupied a very special position. A place of privilege, you might say. Oh, I don't mean that there weren't times when they were looked down upon, and respectability was never truly a part of it; but they always had a path of privilege. They were a sort of class apart from all other classes and they hobnobbed with kings and dukes and all that sort of thing. It gave them a rather distorted view of themselves—oh, all of them, writers, scenic designers, stagehands, actors—and they would find it blurring. You know what I mean—which is the play and which is for real. Am I asleep and dreaming that I am awake, or is it the other way around?"

"Yes, I've had the feeling," Goldstein agreed.

"You've acted?"

"The coffee's delicious," Goldstein said, tasting it. "Yes—when I was a kid, I had three years of summer theater and road show. I know exactly what you mean. You look at the footlights, and there's nothing there but that blur of light, and then your eyes adjust and you see them out there and there's that moment of confusion as to place and part." He closed his eyes a moment, and then he went on, "You don't mind if I go back downstairs, I really think that Cunningham will take Jerry. It never happened before and the money on Cunningham is very attractive. Will you come along?"

I shook my head. Goldstein signed for both of us and then left, and after I sat for a while, I decided to go upstairs to the library. The Mummers' is very old, and the library is still full of overstuffed leather chairs and nineteenth-century portraits. There were five members there, all of them the older type and therefore very much like myself. Two of them nodded and the others never looked up from their reading. I dropped into one of the big chairs, trying to think of something I wanted very much to read—but my interest had lagged, and the night had been so long that now finally I felt weary and hardly able to keep my eyes open. I was dozing when I heard the kind of distant crash that might have come from a tall building shaken badly, so that its brickwork and stonework tumbles away; but in that nowhere between sleep and awakeness I might have been dreaming.

I opened my eyes then. The other members were still absorbed in their reading.

I leaned back and allowed myself to doze off again. How annoyed I would have been if someone had done that during a scene of one of my own plays! Yet I always had a nod of sympathy for the older folks, many of them lifelong devotees of the theater, who nevertheless caught forty winks during the intermission, when the set was being changed.

the movie house

We had an interval for popcorn and vitamins, and the projectionist came down from above. This did not happen often, and sometimes days would go by without our seeing him. His name was Matthew Ragen, and he was six feet three inches tall, and he made a most imposing presence with his great shock of white hair and his bright blue eyes. Talk had it that he was over eighty years old, but I find that hard to believe, because his stance was very erect and his walk as firm and easy as the walk of a younger man. However, there was no one who could remember a time when he was not the projectionist.

We crowded around him, delighted that he was walking among us. The children tried to touch him, and I am sure that in their fanciful minds they confused him with God. It was a great pleasure and privilege to be sought out by him, greeted by him—or even to be the recipient of his smile; and you can imagine how astonished I was when he came straight toward me, the people parting to let him through, and greeted me personally.

I had to pull myself together before I could speak, and then I simply said, "I am honored, Projectionist."

"Not at all, Dorey. It is I who am honored."

"Have I pleased you, Projectionist?"

"I think you've pleased us all, Dorey."

People listening nodded and smiled, and I think that I guessed what was coming. Was I surprised? Certainly, for no one is ever sure; but perhaps not as surprised as I might have been.

"A special treat, Dorey," the projectionist said. "A Western called *High Noon*. I am sure you remember it."

I nodded with delight, and the people around smiled with pleasure.

"I suppose it's ten years since I have played it," the projectionist went on. "It wants an occasion, you know. It's not something you throw in any old time. Well, we'll run it, Dorey, and then we'll have an interval for announcements."

"Thank you, Projectionist," I said graciously—and as modestly as I could. "Thank you, indeed."

It was something to be singled out by the projectionist; people looked at me differently. It not only gave one status, but added to the status a delicious feeling of self-importance that made one literally glow with pleasure. Jane, Clarey, Lisa, Mona—these were girls I had sat with on and off for years; suddenly their whole attitude toward me was different, and Jane tried to take possession. She was pushy; I realized that now, and how easily I could dispense with her. But more than that, I wanted to sit alone. I wanted to be by myself and within myself while I watched *High Noon*. I was sure the projectionist had a very good reason for playing it, and I wanted to concentrate and understand. I sought out a place in a rear corner of the orchestra, a place frequented mostly by the older people, and while the people around knew me, they would not bother me or intrude upon my privacy.

I relaxed in the chair and entered the world of good and evil—which was the sum and substance of our own place. Gary Cooper was good, and he slew what was evil, which was right. It was not easy. He was a leader who stood alone, because his quality was leadership—and thus I understood why the projectionist had chosen this film. The leader must see right and wrong clearly, and if death is the only solution, the leader must use death even as God would. My heart went out to Gary Cooper. I knew him. He was my brother.

The picture ended, and the deep, rich voice of the projectionist came over the stereo system:

"Let us join in silent prayer. Let us pray that God gives us wisdom in our choices."

I prayed, and then the lights came up. Everyone was alert and eager, and the old folks around me smiled at me. Sister Evelyn, in her function of chairman of the Board of Elections, came onto the stage, and standing there in front of the huge silver screen—so small in front of it—she waited for the chatter of voices to cease. Then she cleared her throat, clapped her hands once or twice for attention, and then said:

"The results are tabulated."

People smiled, and heads turned, twisting around and up toward the projection booth. They wanted the projectionist to know. You must understand that we very often and quietly discussed the projectionist. If the Godhead made the film, then surely the projectionist was of the nature of God. No one actually declared this as a firm proposition; but on the other hand, neither had we ever heard of a birth date for the projectionist.

Sister Evelyn clapped her hands again. "Will Dorey please rise," she said.

I stood up. I had chosen an obscure corner, so at first people looked vainly here and there for me. Then the whispers located me, and now as I stood, every face in the theater turned toward me.

"Would you approach, Dorey," Sister Evelyn said.

I went to the aisle and walked toward the stage, and meanwhile Sister Evelyn was telling the people by what vote I had won the election. It was a very decent majority. Well, for ten years I had dreamed of being president and had prayed for the honor. Now it had come. I stood on the stage, and Al Hoppner, the retiring president, joined us, and he took off his great ribbon and medallion of honor and placed it around my neck, the broad blue band coming over my shoulders and the shining medallion bright against my breast. Then the people gave me a standing ovation, cheering and clapping for fully four minutes. I timed it surreptitiously, raising my hand in a sort of acknowledgment and noting the time on my wristwatch. I knew that Al Hoppner's ovation had lasted only two and a half minutes, so this was in the way of underwriting a change and a statement of trust in my own sense of responsibility.

I would choose two assistants, and the three of us would constitute the Committee, and the plain truth of it was that I had been mulling over my choices for more than a week—ever since the vote and the possibility that I would be elected president. Now I named Schecter and Kiley. Schecter was in his late thirties, a solid and dependable man who had worked in this post before. He was not a leader, but he was a born committeeman, and he would remain a committeeman for the rest of his life. Kiley was something else. Kiley was only twenty-one years old, and this was the first post of responsibility that he had ever held. He had manifested leadership qualities, and he had wit and imagination. I felt proud of myself for choosing him and standing by him, even though the cheers of the audience were rather muted. Naturally, people suspect youth.

Finally we left the platform and the projectionist began one of those splendid color spectacles—I think this was called *The Robe*—and it drew the people immediately into that part of the world known as Ancient Rome.

For myself, Schecter, and Kiley, we had work to do, and we would thereby forego this discovery. (I must mention here that the projectionist frowned on the word "film" to describe what took place on the great silver screen. He preferred to call it "discovery" in terms of a view or discovery of another part of the great world we inhabited.)

We would, instead, begin immediately to inventory and check supplies—this being one of the prime duties of the president. Coming into my administration, I had to assess the condition of place and things; and then I would make my report to the people.

Naturally, we checked the popcorn first, and then the quantity and freshness of the butter. Sadie and Lackaday and Milty were in charge of popcorn and butter, but they closed shop whenever one of the large spectacles opened. They were a bit provoked now at having to remain and watch us check out their duties and answer whatever questions we asked them; but I had decided to lay down the law immediately. I would show an iron hand and make my position on law and order plain—and thereby they would stop thinking that since I had made so radical a choice in Kiley, I would be soft and wishy-washy. In this instance I kept Kiley with me, working steadily, firmly, and in an organized fashion, so that he too could get an idea of how my administration would proceed. Meanwhile, I sent Schecter to root out the ushers and line them up in the lobby.

The ushers were prone to relax and slip into last-row seats whenever any discovery interested them, and that was one of the many slipshod things that I intended to stop. I had left Kiley to finish up with the popcorn and butter and was making my first cursory survey of the candy bars when I glimpsed the ushers marching through to the lobby.

I had not been wrong in my choice of Schecter. When I came into the lobby, the ushers were lined up in a military formation that would have done credit to West Point. I walked up and down their ranks, studying them meticulously, and I must confess that their uniforms were somewhat less admirable than their formation and posture—buttons left unbuttoned, collars open, trousers that had long lost their creases, and some even were without hats. I addressed them, stressing first how pleased I was with their military formation and posture and informing them of my high opinion of Schecter, who, among his many duties, would have that of being commanding officer of the ushers.

"However," I said, "let no one imagine that I will tolerate slovenliness or disorder. A disorderly uniform denotes a disorderly mind, and I will not have it in an organization upon which our very existence depends. Do not imagine that you can deceive or befuddle either Schecter or myself. We will parade again tomorrow morning, and I want to see you appear as ushers should appear."

For the next three days we continued to check and inventory popcorn, butter, candy bars, soda pop, and cigarettes. My choice of Kiley appeared then to be a brilliant one; for while Schecter was whipping the ushers into shape, Kiley had gone to work on three hot-drink, ice-cream, and cigarette machines that had not been functioning for months. Kiley had a really extraordinary grasp of mechanics, and he had found a room opening off the lobby that was unused and where he decided to establish a machine shop of sorts. The room had another door—one of the locked doors. Kiley was very young, and he had never actually realized that locked doors existed.

He had called me to see the room and to give him permission to use it, and he met me at the entrance to the lobby and took me there.

"Oh, yes," I said. "I know this room, Kiley. It was once called the office, although it has not been used for any purpose for years."

"For some reason I find it very exciting."

"Oh?"

"You know, I haven't looked at the screen for days, Dorey. It's very strange not to participate in the discoveries. It gives me an odd feeling. Do you know what I mean?"

"Not really, no."

"Just some silly notion," Kiley said, rather embarrassed. He pointed across the room. "Have you noticed that door? I wonder where it leads to?"

"It's a locked door."

"You mean—an actual locked door?"

"Exactly."

"Well, what do you know!" Kiley exclaimed. He was absolutely delighted. "A real locked door. Do you know, I never believed they existed."

"You never believed it?"

"No, I always thought it was some sort of metaphysical nonsense."

"Well, there it is," I said. There were a good many locked doors, and I found it rather strange that anyone should doubt their existence. However, Kiley was very young, and one tended to lose touch with what the young knew or did not know.

Kiley walked over to the door, studied it, tried the handle, and then turned to me and said eagerly, his bright blue eyes wide and excited:

"Why don't we open it, Dorey?"

"What?"

"I said, why don't we open the locked door?"

"Kiley, Kiley," I said patiently, "the door is locked."

"I know. But we could open it."

"How?"

"With a key."

"A what?"

"A key, Dorey—a key!"

"Bless your heart, Kiley, there is no such thing as a key."

"But there must be."

"No, Kiley, there is not. A locked door is a locked door, and nothing can change that."

"But a key could."

"Kiley, I told you that there is no such thing as a key. I know that the word exists, but it is only a symbol, a metaphysical symbol. I may not be a particularly devout man, Kiley, but I have always been on the side of religion, and I don't think that anyone will doubt my dedication to the religious establishment. Nevertheless, I must state that metaphysics is one thing and reality is something entirely different. I tell you flatly that a key is like a miracle. We talk of them; some even believe in them; but I have never found anyone who has ever seen one. Do you understand?"

Kiley nodded slowly.

"Then I suggest we forget about keys and set to turning this room into an adequate machine shop, and if we do, we ought to have those vending machines in tip-top shape very soon. Do you agree, Kiley?"

"Yes—yes, of course."

"And quite a number of other things need repairing. Some of the chairs in the theater are absolutely unfit to sit on."

"Yes, sir," Kiley said.

The projectionist had announced a Swedish sex film for that night, and I told Schecter and Kiley that they could have the evening for the discovery, since they had been working quite hard and since it was not too often that the projectionist permitted a sex film. Schecter licked his lips with pleasure—a dirty old man if there ever was one—but Kiley said that he would prefer to tinker around in the machine shop, if I didn't mind. You can't fault devotion to duty, and of course I said that I didn't mind. I had already made my own arrangements with a delightful little blonde called Baba, and we met before the lights went off. Whenever we had a sex film, the projectionist insisted on blacking out the theater. It made a sort of sense, for the older folks are embarrassed by the close presence of younger people during a sex film, and certainly the young are made uneasy by the presence of their parents. So the auditorium was blacked out, and ushers, using tiny hand flashlights, took us to our seats.

There has been a great deal of discussion, pro and con, concerning sex on the screen; and even though the puritanical elements have considerable power, the decision was always made to continue with sex discoveries. I felt that this was because the puritans enjoyed them even more than the others; and also I might add that sex films play an important role in the reproductive activities that serve to perpetuate our society. I certainly enjoy those rare evenings, and this time I felt sorry for Kiley.

I must say that I was rather kind to him the following day. I went out of my way to compliment him on his inventories of the candy, and he in turn took me into his machine shop, which I praised highly. He was constructing a sort of lathe, which, as he explained, would enable him to reproduce elements of the vending machines.

"And do you know, Mr. President, sir," he said eagerly, "I think I could use the same machine to make a key."

"Kiley!" I said.

"Yes, sir—I know how you feel about keys."

"Not how I feel, Kiley. It's how the world feels."

"Yes, sir," Kiley said very seriously. "I know that. I am ready to accept how the world feels. I mean I don't want you to feel that I'm a radical or anything of that sort—"

"I don't, Kiley. Rest assured that if I did, I never would have appointed you to the Committee. You are very young to be a member of the Committee, Kiley."

"I know that, sir."

"But I had confidence in you."

"Yes, sir."

"I had confidence in your stability, your judgment."

"Thank you, Dorey. I'm very flattered that you took such an interest in me."

"But above all, I want you to consider me as a friend."

"Oh, I do," Kiley said earnestly.

"Then as a friend, Kiley, I must ask you to give up this delusion about keys."

"Do you consider it harmful, sir—I mean to think about it or plan to make one?"

"To make something that doesn't exist?"

"But people do. I mean they make something that doesn't exist."

"Not keys, Kiley."

"Sir?"

"Why must you argue with me, Kiley? Some of the wisest men in our society have gone into this question of keys. There are no keys. There never were. There never will be."

Kiley stared at me, his honest, boyish eyes wide open.

"Yes, Kiley. I want you to promise me something."

"Sir?"

"That you will never mention this matter of keys again. Forget it. Put it out of your mind. There is no such thing as a key. There never was. There never will be."

"Yes, sir."

"Good lad." I squeezed his shoulder affectionately—to show him that I bore no ill will toward him. "Now I want you to get to work on those vending machines. You have no idea how much the people miss hot chocolate. Especially the older folks. It appears to be one of few consolations of old age."

"I will."

"When might you have them?"

"Two weeks—three at the very most."

"Good. Excellent. But all work and no play makes Jack a dull boy, and I want you to take this evening off. The projectionist is showing a very rare and special piece called *Little Caesar*, which dates back to the time when organized hoodlums challenged city government. It is restricted to those who are in government today or have served in government in the past."

"Thank you, sir," Kiley answered enthusiastically.

It was Kiley's very quality of being outgoing and enthusiastic that threw me off the track. It was difficult to think of anyone with his spontaneous quality as being a creature of duplicity, but there is no other label for his subsequent actions; and five days later the whole thing exploded in my face.

Schecter came to me with it. "Dorey," he said grimly, "the devil's at work."

"Oh?"

"You know I am not prone to exaggeration."

"I know that."

"Well, I saw Kiley enter his shop today."

"What's so unusual about that?"

"I wanted a word with him."

"So?"

"I followed him. I opened the door to his office and entered. He wasn't there."

"Perhaps he left before you got there."

"I told you I saw him enter his shop. I watched the door to his shop—the door that opens into the lobby. I saw him go in. I never took my eyes off that door until I opened it. No one came out of his shop. No one."

"Then he was in there," I said calmly.

"Damnit, Dorey—am I an idiot? The room was empty."

"How could it have been empty? You said you never took your eyes off the door."

"Exactly. Still it was empty."

"All right," I sighed. "Suppose we both look into this. There are no devils, no keys, no miracles—I made all that very clear to Kiley, so suppose we just look into this."

"Good," Schecter agreed, his jaw set firmly. "Good."

He led the way into the lobby, and as we reached there, he signaled for a squad of ushers to follow us. When we reached the door to Kiley's workshop, I said to Schecter:

"Really, do we need them?"

"Alertness is the first rule of military practice! They're ushers, Dorey! This is their place, their duty! Man for man, I will match them against any dirty little subversive that ever lived!"

"Oh, come on now, Schecter—we're not going to call Kiley a subversive."

"If the name fits—"

"There's no indication that it fits or that Kiley did anything wrong. Let's have a look."

I opened the door to the workshop. I had not been inside the place in days, but Kiley's lathe was finished, and on his worktable were the bright new pieces for the vending machine. Kiley himself was not there.

"Well?" Schecter demanded.

I went out into the lobby and said to the ushers: "Did Kiley come through the lobby during the past hour?"

They shook their heads.

I went back into the workshop and closed the door behind me. Standing there now, alone with Schecter, I allowed my eyes to wander over the place again and again. It was a small room and there was no place to hide, no nook, no corner, no cranny.

"Well, sir, are you satisfied?" Schecter demanded.

"I'll let you know when I'm satisfied, Schecter."

He allowed himself a slight smile of satisfaction, and I went to the other door and tried it.

"That's a locked door, Dorey," Schecter informed me.

"I know bloody damn well that it's a locked door."

"Well, I just thought—"

"I don't give two damns what you thought, Schecter. Let's get out of here."

Schecter paraded out of the room into the lobby where the ushers were waiting, and I followed him, closing the door behind me. At that moment I heard a sound inside the shop, and I said to Schecter, "You wait out here. I'm going back in there."

I turned and opened the door of Kiley's shop again, slipped through, and closed it behind me before Schecter could squirm around and see what I was up to. Kiley was inside the shop now, grinning with delight and excitement, holding a small piece of shining metal in his hand.

"Kiley," I cried, "where the hell were you?"

"Outside."

"What do you mean, outside?"

"Through that door." He pointed to the locked door.

"What? Are you crazy? That's a locked door. No one goes through a locked door!"

"I did."

I held up my hand and pointed a shaking finger at him. "Kiley, have you gone off your nut? Have you lost your mind? You're talking crazy. You're talking so goddamn crazy even I won't be able to protect you. You talk about going through a locked door. A locked door is locked. No one goes through it."

"I unlocked it," Kiley said, almost squealing with delight.

"You unlocked it," I said with cold, deliberate scorn. "Only the greatest minds of our time have given their attention to locked doors and have proved that they can never be unlocked—but you unlocked it, all by yourself."

"And with a key!" Kiley cried. "You said I couldn't make a key, but I did. Here it is." He held up the little piece of metal, coming toward me and offering it to me.

"Keep your distance! Keep that damn thing away from me! I told you there is no such thing as a key!"

"But here it is—here it is, Dorey. Believe me, I unlocked the door and I went outside—" He turned and pointed toward the locked door. "Out there, through the locked door. My God almighty, Kiley, out there the sun is shining in such a blaze of golden glory that the mind can't conceive it, and there's green grass and green trees and tall buildings, and people—thousands and thousands of people, real people who wear bright-colored clothes and the sun splashes down over them, and the girls have long, bare legs and brown and yellow and black hair, and they're real, Dorey, real! Not like those shadows that the projectionist shows us on the big screen. Do you think his discoveries are real or even discoveries? They're not. They're shadows, lies, illusions—but outside that door the world is real—"

"Enough!" I screamed at him. "God damn you, enough!"

I flung open the door to the lobby and yelled, "Schecter! Schecter—get here on the double with your damn ushers!"

Schecter and the ushers poured into the little room, grabbing Kiley and overwhelming him. Kiley didn't struggle; he just stared at me in astonishment and with such hurt surprise that I said:

"Oh, for Christ's sake, Schecter, let go of him."

"What?"

"I said leave him alone and get your damned ushers out of here—now."

"Didn't you just call me?"

"You give me a pain in the ass, Schecter. Get out of here and take your ushers with you."

Aggrieved, scowling, looking hate at Kiley and me, Schecter led the ushers out of the room; and then I turned tiredly to Kiley and said:

"You certainly do louse things up, don't you? Here I go out on a limb to make you the youngest committeeman ever, and what do I get in return? A raving lunatic, that's what I get in return."

"Dorey, I'm not a raving lunatic."

"Then what in hell are you?"

"I went outside. I saw—"

"Shut up."

Kiley clenched his lips, and I said to him, "Kiley, let me make this clear. No one opens a locked door. There are no keys, and you did not go outside."

"Then what is this?" he demanded, holding up the bit of metal he had in his hand.

"A bit of metal. Nothing. There are no keys. There is no outside."

"Oh, Dorey, I went outside."

"You know what?" I said to him. "I'll tell you what, Kiley. You did not go out. You went nowhere. Now if you can get that through your head—if you can only admit that this whole thing of yours is a lie and an invention, well, then, maybe we can work something out. Maybe. Maybe not. But maybe."

"My God, Dorey, do you know what you're asking me to do?"

"To stop lying."

"You were in this room before?" Kiley demanded.

"Yes."

"Schecter too."

"Damnit, yes! So what?"

"Was I here? That's what I'm getting at, Dorey. Was I here?"

"No!" I almost shouted.

"Then where was I?"

"How the hell do I know where you were?"

"All right," Kiley said. "All right, Dorey. Then give me a chance. That's all I'm asking for. Let me open that locked door. I worked it out, and I made this key. I got it right here in my hand." He held it up for me to see. "Let me use it, Dorey. Let me open the door. Let me take you out there."

"No!"

"Why?"

"Because there is no such thing as a key and because you can't open a locked door."

"Then I will—" And he whirled and started toward the locked door.

"Kiley!" My voice hit him like a whiplash. I meant it to. He hesitated, and I snapped at him. "Kiley—take one more step and I call Schecter and his ushers."

He turned to me, pleading, "Why? Why?"

"Because there is no outside, Kiley. Because you're a twisted, pathological personality. Now, for the last time, Kiley—will you admit that you are fantasying?"

"No."

"Then you'll have to come with me to the projectionist, Kiley. Will you come willingly, or must I call Schecter?"

"Oh, God, Dorey, won't you let me open that damn door—just a crack—just so you could see the blaze of sunshine?"

"No."

"Please—must I get down on my knees, Dorey?"

"No. Now is it the ushers, or do you come peacefully?"

"I'll go with you, Dorey," Kiley said, defeated now, his shoulders hanging, the light gone from his eyes.

Somehow, word had gotten around, and there were people in the lobby who watched silently as we came through. Kiley was well liked, and only Schecter and his ushers regarded him with hate. I took Kiley into the theater and through it to the stairs. It was children's time, and today that meant a series of twelve Bugs Bunny cartoons. The children were clapping and cheering, and as we passed by the back row, Kiley said:

"Why can't you think of how it would be for them outside, Dorey?"

"Still on that. What will you say to the projectionist?"

"The truth."

"Yes. He'll appreciate that."

We were outside the projectionist's booth now, far up above the second balcony. No one ever entered the booth. Instead, you pressed a button and then spoke into a speaking tube.

"I'm terribly busy now, Dorey—putting together a whole new part of the world, you know, the Fitzgerald travelogues. Thus we have not only discoveries but explorations. So if it could wait?"

"I am afraid not, Projectionist."

"Urgent?"

"Yes, Projectionist."

"If you might hint at the nature of the emergency, Dorey?"

"It's young Kiley."

"Your committeeman?"

"Yes, Projectionist. He claims to have opened a locked door."

"Of course you have told him that locked doors can never be opened—that this is the way God made the world?"

"I told him."

"Dear me. Well, go to my office. You have him with you?"

"Yes."

"Is he docile?"

"He won't give us any trouble, Projectionist."

"Good. Go to my office and wait there for me, Dorey."

"Yes, Projectionist."

I took Kiley to his office then. The projectionist's office was on the same level as the projection booth, but at the far end of the theater. We went in and sat in the leather armchairs, and while we were waiting there an usher came up with popcorn and frozen ice-cream balls and hot coffee. He would have brought the projectionist his supper now, and the projectionist had sent down for additional food for Kiley and myself. That was so like the projectionist, gentle and considerate of all the needs of others.

"Are you afraid?" I asked Kiley. After all, he was only a kid, and it was to be expected that he would be afraid.

"No. Well, maybe a little."

"You mustn't be. It's in the hands of the projectionist now."

"What will he do to me, Dorey?"

"I don't know, but whatever he does, it will be the right thing. You can count on the projectionist for that. He's very wise. When he makes a decision, it's a just decision, believe me."

"Yes, I guess so."

"No guessing, Kiley. Rest assured. If you will only get these damn fantasies out of your head."

Then the projectionist entered, and we both rose to our feet in respect. He nodded pleasantly and told us to be seated. He walked around to the back of his big desk and sat down in a big swivel chair, the kind that judges use on the bench.

"So this is young Kiley," he said amiably. "Fine-looking lad. I knew your father, Kiley. Good man—yes, indeed. And your grandfather. Good people, good family." And then to me, "What seems to be the trouble, Dorey?"

"I would prefer that Kiley told you himself."

"Do that, Kiley," the projectionist said.

"Yes, Projectionist." Kiley's voice trembled slightly, but that was not unusual when people first met the projectionist. "You see, Dorey let me set up a small machine shop in that unused room off the lobby. I made a lathe to cut out some new parts for the vending machines. There was a locked door in the room, and I thought I might make a key on the lathe and open the locked door—"

"I'm sure you didn't consider that," the projectionist interrupted. "You know that locked doors can never be opened. That's the nature of the world, the way God made it."

"I thought that if I made a key, Projectionist—"

"A key? Poor Kiley. There are no keys, no dragons, no unicorns, no magicians. God has ordered His world in the best of possible ways. Myths are for children."

"But I made the key and opened the door and went out into the world, Projectionist."

"Don't excite yourself, Kiley."

"But you must listen to me and believe me."

"Ah, yes. We do believe you, Kiley. Of course we do."

"Then you do! You do believe me."

"Oh, yes."

"And you know that everything in here is of shadows—without any meaning or substance, and all that is real and beautiful is outside?"

"Yes, Kiley."

"And what will we do?" Kiley asked with great excitement. "Will we go out of here? Have we been waiting only for a time, a moment—as if for God to reach down and touch us and open our eyes? Then there would be some meaning in our own life, wouldn't there? In my life? Oh, I never dreamed to be such an instrument. Thank you, Projectionist, thank you, thank you."

"It is nothing, Kiley," the projectionist said gently, while I stared at him in astonishment. "You deserve many things, and they will come to you. Now wait here for a little while. Dorey and I must step outside and have a few words in private concerning this momentous happening. You understand?"

With tears in his eyes Kiley nodded and then he said to me, "Believe me, Dorey, I hold nothing against you. How could you know? How could anyone know without seeing it with his own two eyes? I mean anyone but the projectionist. He knew. He knew immediately. Didn't you, sir?"

"Immediately," the projectionist agreed.

"God bless you!" Kiley exclaimed. "I shouldn't be saying that to anyone so superior to me as yourself, but I must say it. God bless you, Projectionist."

"Thank you, my lad. Now wait here in peace. Dorey, come with me."

Still speechless and astonished, I followed the projectionist out into the hall, where he whispered sharply, "Get that stupid expression off your face, Dorey. You're the President."

"But I thought, Projectionist–"

"I know what you thought. I simply dissembled in front of the poor lad. His mind is gone and his disease is serious and infectious. He must be put away, you know."

"Put away?"

"Yes, Dorey–put away."

"Where?"

"In the subcellar, Dorey, deep down in the old coalpit."

"Forever?"

"I imagine so."

"Can't he be cured?"

"Not of this particular delusion, Dorey. He is like a man

who believes that he has seen the face of God. The vision becomes more than the man."

"I hate to do it."

"Do you imagine I like it?"

"Is there no other possible way, Projectionist?"

"None."

The projectionist went back to his booth, and I went down to Schecter and told him what we had to do. He smiled and licked his lips with pleasure, and believe me, I could have killed him then and there, but being a President entails certain duties, and there is no way to avoid them. So I let Schecter be and instead faced the look on Kiley's face when we walked into the projectionist's office and arrested him, binding his hands in back of him.

"Dorey, you can't get away with this!" he shouted. "You heard what the projectionist said to me."

"I do this at his order," I replied dully.

"No. No, you're lying."

"I'm not lying, Kiley. God help me, I am not lying."

"But why would he go back on his own word?"

"He was humoring you."

Kiley began to weep. We took him down, balcony to balcony, and then into the basement. It was fortunate for all of us that the projectionist had begun the Fitzgerald travelogues, for everyone was in the theater now. They were of the nature of the world. How can man live and not be filled with curiosity about his world? As unhappy as I was for Kiley's fate, I was also somewhat irritated that because of him I would miss the beginning of the travelogues. Still, duty is duty.

The coalpit was the fourth level under the orchestra, a dark, low-ceilinged part of the basement. A great iron hinged cover had to be lifted, and then we untied Kiley's hands, knotted a rope around his waist, and lowered him down into the coalpit.

"It's there!" he screamed up at me. "Dorey, it's there! Do you think you can destroy it by destroying me?"

And then the iron cover clanged shut. Poor Kiley!

the insects

People heard about the first transmission in various ways. Although unidentified radio appeals are fairly frequent and not generally subject to any general news dissemination—being more or less of oddities and often the work of cranks—they are not jealously guarded. The interesting part of this signal was that it had been repeated at least two dozen times and had been picked up in various parts of the world in various languages, in Russian in Moscow, in Chinese in Peking, in English in New York and London, in Swedish in Stockholm. In all these various places it was on the high-frequency band, somewhat less than twenty-five megacycles.

We heard about it from Fred Goldman, who runs the monitor room for the National Broadcasting Company, when he and his wife dined with us early in May. He has his ear to things; he listens to the whole damn world breathing in a half a dozen languages, and he likes to drop things, like a ship at sea pleading for help and then silence and not one word in the press, or a New Orleans combination playing the latest hard rock—if such a thing is possible—in Yarensk, which is somewhere in the tundra of Northern Siberia, or any other of a dozen incongruous daily happenings across the radio waves of the earth. But on this night he was rather suppressed and thoughtful, and when he came out with it, it was less odd than reasonable.

"You know," he said, "there was a sort of universal complaint today and we can't pinpoint it."

"Oh?"

My wife poured drinks. His own wife looked at him sharply, as if this was the first she had heard of it and she resented being put on parity with us.

"Good, clear signal," he said. "High frequency. Queer voice though—know what it said?"

There was another couple there—the Dennisons; he was a rather important surgeon—and Mrs. Dennison made a rather inept attempt at humor. I try to remember her first name, but it escapes me. She was a slim, beautiful blonde woman, but not very bright; yet she managed to turn it on Fred and he retreated. We tried to persuade him, but he turned the subject away and became a listener. It wasn't until after dinner that I pinned him down.

"About that signal?"

"Oh, yes."

"You've become damn sensitive."

"Oh, I don't know. Nothing very special or mysterious. A voice said, 'You must stop killing us.'"

"Just that?"

"It doesn't surprise you?" Fred asked.

"Oh, no—hardly. As you said, it's a sort of universal plea. I can think of at least seven places on earth where those would be the most important words they could broadcast."

"I suppose so. But it did not originate in any of those places."

"No? Where, then?"

"That's it," Fred Goldman said. "That's just it."

That's how I heard about it first. I put it out of mind as I imagine so many others did, and the truth is that I forgot about it. Two weeks later I delivered the second lecture in the Goddard Free Series at Harvard, and during the question period one student demanded:

"What is your own reaction, Dr. Cornwall, to the curtain of silence the Establishment has thrown around the radio messages?"

I was naïve enough to ask what messages he referred to, and a ripple of laughter told me that I was out of it.

"'You must stop killing us.' Isn't that it, Dr. Cornwall?" the boy shouted, and more applause greeted this than I had gotten on my own. "Isn't that the crux of it?" the student went on. "'You must stop killing us'—isn't that it?"

I took a brandy afterward with Dr. Fleming, the dean, in front of the fire in his own warm and comfortable study, and he mentioned that the university did a certain amount of monitoring of sorts. "The kids weren't too disturbing, were they?" he asked.

I assured him that I agreed with them. "We're both Establishment of sorts," I said, "so I don't want to wriggle out of it. But isn't that the radio signal? A friend of mine was telling me something about it. Did it come across again?"

"Every day now," the dean said. "The kids have taken it up as a sort of battle cry."

"But I saw nothing in the papers."

"That's curious, isn't it?" Fleming said. "I suppose some

wraps are being put on it in Washington, although I can't imagine why."

"They couldn't locate the source the first day."

"We've tried on our own, and they've tried even harder over at M.I.T. It's plaintive enough, but of what import I don't know. Only the student body is very hot about it."

"So I noticed," I agreed.

A few days later at breakfast my wife informed me that she had lunched the previous day with Rhoda Goldman. The information was dropped like a small, careful bomb.

"Go on," I said with great interest.

"You'll pooh-pooh it."

"Try me."

"They have some background on the signals down at the station. Or at least they think they have."

"Oh?"

"They think they know who is sending them."

"Thank God for that. Maybe we can stop killing them—or stop whoever is doing the killing. It's the most God-awful plaintive thing I ever heard of."

"No."

"No?"

"I said no, we can't stop," my wife replied very seriously, "because it's the insects."

"What?"

"That's what Rhoda Goldman said—insects. They are sending the messages."

"I am pooh-poohing it," I agreed.

"I knew you would," my wife said.

I have been on four of the mayor's special committees, and

the following day his assistant called and asked me whether I would serve on another. However, he refused to spell out the purpose, except to say that it was connected with the high-frequency messages.

"Surely you've heard of them," he said.

I agreed that I had heard of them and I agreed to serve on the committee, chiefly out of curiosity. The day I went down-town for the meeting of the new committee was the same day that General Carl de Hargod, the new chief of staff, had arrived in New York to address a dinner group at the Waldorf; and now he was being welcomed at City Hall by both the mayor and about a thousand pickets. The pickets were a conglomeration of pacifist groups and hippies, and they marched back and forth in front of City Hall in silence, carrying signs which read: "You must stop killing us."

I had arrived early enough to get inside just before the welcoming ceremonies began, and when I joined the others of the newly formed committee I listened to an apology for the mayor's absence and an assurance that he would be with us within the half hour. There were five others on the committee, three men and two women. I knew both women, Kate Gordon, who was Commissioner of Health, and Alice Kinderman, who was associated with the Museum of Natural History and newly named consultant to the Parks Department, and one of the men—Frank Meyers, a lawyer with important contacts in Washington. Meyers introduced me to the others, Basehart, who was the head of the Department of Entomology in the huge City University, and Krummer, from the Department of Agriculture in Washington.

It was the presence of the entomologist that bounced off

my mind incredulously, and when Meyers asked me whether I knew what we had been gathered together for, I replied only that it had something to do with the radio signals.

"The point is, we know who is sending them."

"What is," Alice Kinderman amended. *"Who is* is rather disturbing."

"I don't believe it," I said. "I prefer the communists."

"We have been killing a good many communists," Basehart agreed, with that curious detachment of a scientist. "I'm sure they don't like it. Well, no one likes to be killed, do they? This time it's the insects, however."

"Fudge!" said Kate Gordon.

Then we talked about it, calmly, in a manner befitting the six middle-aged, civilized men and women that we were, and if there were doubters among us, Basehart convinced them. He convinced me. He was a small, long-nosed man with electric blue eyes and an exciting smile. Anyone could see that what had happened was, so far as he was concerned, the most wonderful and exciting thing that had ever happened, and as he explained it, the preposterous disappeared and the inevitable took over. He convinced us that it had been inevitable all along. The only thing he could not persuade us to do was to share his enthusiasm.

"It's so logical," he maintained. "The insect is not a thing in itself but a fragment. The hive is the thing. Insects don't think in our terms; they don't have brains. At best they have something that might be thought of as one of these printed circuits we make for mass-produced radios. They are cells, not organs. But does the hive think? Does the swarm think? Does the city of insects think? That's the question we have never been able to answer satisfactorily. And what of the super-swarm? We have always known that they communicate with each other and with the swarm or the hive. But how? Certainly some sort of wave—and why not high frequency?"

"Power?" someone asked.

"Power. My goodness—have you any notion as to how many of them there are? Of species alone—almost half a million. Of individuals—beyond our ability to compute. They could generate any power required. Accomplish any task—if of course they come together into the theoretical super-hive or super-swarm and become conscious of themselves. And it appears they have. You know, we've always killed them, but now perhaps too many of them. They have a great instinct for survival."

"And we seem to have lost ours somewhere along the line, haven't we?" I wondered.

The mayor had too many responsibilities, too many problems in a city that was close to unmanageable, and it was difficult to say how seriously he took the plea of the insects. People in public life tend to become defensive about such things. I had lectured often enough on questions of social ecology to know how difficult it was to impress political leadership with the possibility that we may just be working ourselves out of a livable future.

"We have just had to arrest over a hundred pacifists," the mayor said tiredly, "most of them from good families—which means I will not sleep tonight, and since I had only an hour or two last night, I think you will understand my reluctance, ladies and gentlemen, to become excited about radio messages sent by insects. I give it credence only because the Department of Agriculture insists that I do—and so I ask you to please serve on this very ad hoc committee and draw up a report on the matter. We are allocating five thousand dollars for clerical assistance, and we have also been promised the full cooperation of the Ford Foundation."

The mayor could not remain with us, but we spent another half hour chatting about the matter, arranged for our next meeting, and then went our several ways. Belief in the absurd is not very tenacious, and I think that by the time our meeting broke up, we had put away the insects under a solid cover of doubt. With many pressures, I had half forgotten the matter by dinnertime, when my wife asked me pertly:

"Well, Alan—what will you do about the insects?"

When I did not answer immediately, my wife informed me that she had been on the phone that afternoon for almost an hour with her sister, Dorothy, from Upper Montclair, and that they were taking it very seriously indeed. In fact, Dorothy's son, a physics major at M.I.T., had worked out the electronics—or the physics; she couldn't say for certain—underlying the high-frequency signals.

"He's a bright boy," I said.

"And that's a very enlightening comment."

"Well, the mayor formed a committee. I have the honor to be a part of it."

"That's just what I adore most about our handsome mayor," Jane said. "He does have a committee for everything, doesn't he? I'm sure his conscience is clear now—"

"Good heavens," I said, "must he have a conscience about this too—"

I never finished my defense of a poor, harassed man. The telephone rang. It was Bert Clegmann, who was one of the editors of *The New York Times* and whom I knew slightly, and he informed me that they had decided to break the story in their morning edition, since it had already appeared in London and in Rome, and could I tell him anything about the committee?

I told him about the committee, and then I asked him my question.

"Do I believe it?" Clegmann said. "Well, thank heavens I don't have to put my own opinion on the line. There's apparently enough background now for us to quote some eminent people, and the Russians are taking it seriously enough to raise it in the UN. Next week. Also, the little buggers have eaten three thousand four hundred contiguous acres of wheat in eastern Nebraska. Clean as a whistle. That may simply be a coincidence."

"What little buggers?"

"Locusts."

"Well, isn't that a very old business–I mean they always seem to be devouring something, somewhere, don't they?"

But I couldn't get any commitment from Clegmann. He always felt that he was the articulation of the *Times*, so as to speak, and very wary, but that made him no different from most. It was much too great a strain to believe.

"If you are on a committee," my wife said, "then you must believe it."

"I think that part of the work of the committee is to test the validity of the whole thing."

"Doesn't anyone on the committee believe it?"

"Basehart, perhaps. He's an entomologist."

"I feel silly," my wife said, smiling, "but I have been watching the water bugs. They're such huge, dreadful things anyway–I mean even when they don't resent being killed. But what a horrible thought! We simply take it for granted that anything not human doesn't resent being killed."

At our first formal committee meeting, Krummer, the Department of Agriculture man, touched on the same theme, but he was rather acid-tongued about the humanists. After outlining the new program they had set up in Washington, a three-pronged drive, as he put it, insecticides, poison gas, and radiation, he touched on the position of those sensitive people who held that perhaps we killed too easily.

"Can anyone imagine the disaster that would strike mankind if we should give the insects a free hand! Worldwide starvation—not to mention disease and a matter of discomfort."

He went on to paint a rather ghastly picture, to which only Basehart objected, and mildly at that. Basehart pointed out that man had existed before the time of insecticides and had fed himself very nicely.

"There is a natural balance to this kind of thing—an ecological whole. Insects eat each other and birds eat insects and certain animals join in, and even nature in some mysterious way restrains any part of the circle that gets out of hand. But we have killed the birds without mercy and now we are trying to kill the insects, and we keep chopping pieces out of that ecological circle and heaven knows where it will end."

But the main fact presented to the committee was that the high-frequency messages had stopped, and once that visible manifestation of so unnatural a desire as survival had ceased, the party of doubt took over and proceeded to prove that the public had been hoaxed. Since aside from the single fact of devastation in Nebraska there had been no noticeable change in insect behavior anywhere on earth, the fact of a hoax took hold very readily. We appointed Frank Meyers as a one-man subcommittee to investigate the pros and cons of the matter and to report back to us in two weeks.

"This," I explained to my wife, "is the normal process of a committee—not to find but to lose. We shall lose this crisis in very short order."

"In two weeks we are leaving for Vermont," my wife said.

"We'll adjourn for the summer," I assured her. "That too is the normal business of committees."

When we reconvened two weeks later, both Krummer and Meyers delivered reassuring reports.

With great delight Krummer told us that the Pentagon had joined forces with the Department of Agriculture to produce an insecticide so deadly that a quart of it turned into a fine spray would kill any and all insects in a square mile. However, it was almost as deadly to animal and human existence—a matter they hoped to solve in very short order. But Meyers thought it was all to little purpose.

"The people at the C.I.A.," he said, "are just about decided that the Russians are responsible for the high-frequency hoax. They have secret transmitters all over the place, and it's a part of their overall plan to sow fear and discord in the Free World. More to the point, knowing they had blown it, *Pravda* yesterday published a long article blaming it on us. I have also interviewed twenty-three leading naturalists, and all except one agree that the notion of a collective insect intelligence on a par with the intelligence of man is preposterous."

"Of course, our work isn't wasted," Krummer said. "I mean,

a new insecticide is worth its weight in gold, and since it will in its present form kill men as readily as insects, it joins our arsenal of secret weapons. It's an excellent example of how the various sciences tend to overlap, and I think we can salute it as a vital part of the American Way."

"Who was the scientist who did not agree?" I asked.

"Basehart here," Meyers said.

Basehart smiled modestly and replied, "I don't think I can properly be counted, since I am a member of the committee. Which makes the scientific opinion unanimous. Or at least I think that is how it should go into the record."

"You still think it was the insects?" Mrs. Kinderman asked.

"Oh, yes. Yes, indeed."

"Why?"

"Only because it's logical and exciting," said Basehart, "and you know the Russians are so utterly dreary and unimaginative—they would never think of such an idea, not in a thousand years."

"But a collective intelligence," I objected. "I dislike the word preposterous—but surely rather unbelievable."

"Not at all," Basehart replied, almost apologetically. "It's a concept quite familiar to entomologists, and we have discussed it for generations. I will admit that we use it pragmatically when we run out of more acceptable explanations, but there are so many things about the social insects that do not submit to any other explanation. Naturally, we are dealing here with a far more developed and complex intelligence—but who is to say that this is not a perfectly legitimate line of evolution? We are like little children in our understanding of the manner of evolution, and as for its purpose, why, we haven't even begun to inquire."

"Oh, come now," said Kate Gordon, or snorted would be more descriptive, "you are becoming positively teleological, Dr. Basehart, and among scientists I think that is indefensible."

"Oh?" But Basehart did not desire to battle. "Perhaps." He nodded. "Yet some of us cannot help being just a bit teleological. One doesn't always surmount one's childhood religious training."

"Intellectually, one must," said Kate Gordon primly.

"Basehart," I said, "suppose we were to accept this intelligence, not as a reality, but as a matter for discussion. Should we have cause to fear it? Would it be malignant?"

"Malignant? Oh, no—not at all. That has never been my notion of intelligence. Evil is mediocre and rather stupid. No, wisdom is not a malignancy, quite to the contrary. But whether or not we have to fear them—well, that's something else entirely. I mean, we have not come back with a single response. Oh, I don't mean us on this committee. I talk of mankind. Mankind moved only in two directions, to convince itself that an insect intelligence did not exist and to make a new insecticide. But they ask us to stop killing them. What are they to do?"

"Come now"—Meyers laughed—"aren't we playing the game too well? We have been a committee of sincere and interested citizens, and I don't think we have shirked the problem. I move that we adjourn now and reconvene in September."

The motion was seconded and carried.

DRIVING UP TO OUR SUMMER PLACE in Vermont, my wife, Jane, said rather sadly, "If the boy were alive, I wouldn't sleep too well. Do you know, it's three years since he died—and it seems like only yesterday."

"We are beginning a vacation and rest," I told her, "and I will not countenance this kind of mood."

"It's just that I sometimes feel we have stopped caring. Is it a part of growing old?"

"We still care," I said sharply. But I knew exactly what she meant.

Our summer place is in a wonderful, isolated upland valley, like so many of the upland valleys in Vermont, full of sunny days and cool nights and a starry sky over the green folds of earth. It's a place where time moves differently, and after we are there for a while, we move with the time of the place.

We had occasional company, but not too often or too much, and mostly on the weekends. Town was six miles on a dirt road, and twenty miles away was a fair-sized artist colony with a summer symphony and theater and a great many people to talk to if we got lonely. But our visits there were few, two or three times a summer, and we were rarely lonely in the way people understand loneliness. Down the road about a mile lived our nearest neighbor, an old widower named Glenn Olson, who made honey in the summer and maple sugar in the winter. Both were delicious. His maples were old and strong and his bees worked among the wild flowers in the abandoned pastures.

I had been meaning to visit him for both honey and sugar, but put it off from day to day. On the third week the thing happened in the cities. But until then, nothing was very different, only the warm summer days and the birds and the insects humming lazily in the hot air. We could have forgotten the whole thing if only we had disbelieved; but somewhere in both of us was a nugget of belief. We had a postcard from Basehart, who was in the Virgin Islands, where he was cataloguing species and types of insects. The postcard ended with a rather sentimental good-by. Neither my wife nor I remarked on that because, as I said, we had a nugget of belief.

And of course, then, toward the beginning of the summer, the cities died.

There had been a great deal of speculation about the insects and what they might do if they were as some thought. Articles were written, books rushed into print, and even films were planned. There were nightmare things about super-insects, armies of ants, winged devils; but no one anticipated the simple directness of the fact. The insects simply moved against the cities to begin it. Apparently a single intelligence controlled all the movements of the insects, and the millions who perished made no great difference to the survival of the intelligence. They filled the aqueducts and stopped the flow of water. They short-circuited the wires and halted the flow of electricity. They ate the food in the cities and swarmed by the millions over the food coming in. They clogged the valves and intakes of motors and stalled them. They clogged the sewers and they spread disease and the cities died. The insects died by the billions, but this time it was not necessary to kill them. They imposed death on themselves, and the festering, malaria-ridden, plague-ridden cities died with them.

First we watched it happen on television, but the television went very soon. We have a relay tower, and it ceased to function on the third day after the attack on the cities began; after that the picture was so bad as to be meaningless, and a few days later it ceased. We listened to the radio then, until the radio stopped. Then there was the valley as it had always been, and the silence, and the insects hanging in the hot air and the sunlight and the nights.

My own feeling was to drive down to the town, and from day to day I felt that this had to be, but my wife would not have it. Her dread of leaving our place and going to the town was so great that it was not until our food began to run low that she agreed to my going—providing she went with me. Our own telephone had stopped functioning long ago, and it was only after days of not seeing a plane overhead that we realized no planes flew any longer.

Driving down toward town finally, we stopped at Glenn Olson's place, to ask him whether he knew how it was in the village, and perhaps to buy some honey and sugar. We found him in his bedroom, dead—not long dead, perhaps only a day. He had been stung three times on the forearm while he slept. My wife had been a nurse once, and she explained the process whereby three consecutive bee stings would work to kill a man. The air outside was full of bees, humming, working, hanging in the air.

"I think we'll go back to the house," I said.

"We can't leave him like that."

"We can," I said, thinking of how many millions of others were like that.

Olson had a well-stocked cupboard. I filled some bags with canned goods, flour, beans, honey in jars, and maple sugar, and I carried them out to my car, while Jane remained in the house. Then I pulled the blanket over Olson and took Jane by the arm.

"I don't want to go out there," she said.

"Well, we must, you know. We can't stay here."

"I'm afraid."

"But we can't stay here."

Finally I convinced her to come to the car. Her arms were covered and she held a towel over her face, but the bees ignored us. In the car we raised the windows and drove back to our summer place—and then almost ran into our house.

Yet I got over the panic and resisted the temptation to cover myself with mosquito netting. I talked to Jane and finally convinced her that this was not a thing one could avoid or take measures against. It was like the wind, the rain, the sunrise and the sunset. It was happening and nothing we could do would alter it.

"Alan—will it be everyone?" she asked. "Will it be the whole world?"

"I don't know."

"What good would it do them to make it the whole world?"

"I don't know."

"I would not want to live if it were the whole world."

"It's not a question of what we want. It's the way it is. We can only live with it the way it is."

Yet when I went out to the car to bring in the supplies we had taken from Olson's place, I had to call upon every shred of courage and strength I possessed.

It was a little better the next day, and by the third day I convinced Jane to leave the house with me and to walk a little. She covered herself at first, but after a while her fear began to dissipate, and then, bit by bit, it became something you live with—as I suppose anything can. The following week I sat down to write this account. I have been working on it for three days. Yesterday a bee lighted on the back of my hand, a large, fuzzy, working bumblebee. I held my hand firmly and looked at the bee, and the bee returned my stare.

Then the bee flew away, and I had a feeling that it was over and that what would happen had happened. But how we will pick it up and what we will put together, I don't know. I talked about it with my wife last night.

"I hope Basehart is alive and well," she said. "It would be nice to see him again." Which was rather curious, since all she knew about Basehart was what I had told her. Then she began to cry. She was not a woman who cries a great deal, and soon she dried her eyes and took up some sewing that she had laid aside weeks before. I lit my pipe. It was the last of the day. We sat there in silence as darkness fell.

I lit our single kerosene lamp, and she said to me, "We will have to go down to the village sooner or later, won't we?"

"Sooner or later," I agreed.